2012

$, oo

'9

Emily's
Dress
and Other
Missing
Things

Emily's Dress and Other Missing Things

Kathryn Burak

ROARING BROOK PRESS

NEW YORK

In memory of my mother,
Rita Lillian Burak, because
that's where this all starts

Text copyright © 2012 by Kathryn Burak

Published by Roaring Brook Press

Roaring Brook Press is a division of Holtzbrinck Publishing Holdings Limited
Partnership

175 Fifth Avenue, New York, New York 10010

macteenbooks.com

Library of Congress Cataloging-in-Publication Data

Burak, Kathryn.
    Emily's dress and other missing things / Kathryn Burak. — 1st ed.
      p. cm.
    Summary: A new girl in Amherst, Massachusetts, comes to terms with her
mother's suicide and her best friend's disappearance with the help of Emily
Dickinson's poetry—and her dress.
    ISBN 978-1-59643-736-4 (hardcover)
    ISBN 978-1-59643-834-7 (e-book)
    [1. Grief—Fiction.   2. Missing children—Fiction.   3. Dickinson, Emily,
1830–1886—Fiction.   4. Poetry—Fiction.   5. Amherst (Mass.)—Fiction.]
I. Title.

PZ7.B91533Em 2012
[Fic]—dc23

                         2011050246

Roaring Brook Press books are available for special promotions and premiums.
For details contact: Director of Special Markets, Holtzbrinck Publishers.

First edition 2012

Printed in the United States of America

10 9 8 7 6 5 4 3

And then the hunger had more
Power than even sorrow had over me.
—Dante, *Inferno*, XXXIII, 71–72

Love is the distance between you and what you love.
—Meg Hutchinson, "Everything Familiar"

Chapter 1

"This is the window she looked out of every day," the tour guide with the white mustache says. *Step right up, folks, and see that certain slant of light.* Immortality looks like everyday stuff: chairs, doorknobs, Emily Dickinson's white dress on a mannequin, protected by a Plexiglas box.

If you live in Amherst, I recently learned, your English class is required to go to Emily Dickinson's house. You might look around at the old furniture with a sincere appreciation of the day off. But for some people who come here, it's a church. You can see it when they get out of their cars, that they look up the driveway with a light in their eyes. They have come to worship.

"Just look out that window," the tour guide continues, "and you'll start to see what was inside her head."

I look out the window and see trees. *Trees were in her head?*

"We'll go inside her bedroom now, to see the window from which she lowered baskets with candies and cake for the children," the tour guide says.

As if she were fishing for kids, someone whispers. *Creepy.*

"That's horrible."

I look to my left. It's the student teacher from AP English, Mr. Tate, standing right next to me shaking his head, still looking like he just finished the surfing championship—with his golden tan and honey-colored curls. Just the two of us are left, standing in front of the headless mannequin. He's so close to me I can almost identify the brand of his shampoo.

"I don't think it's right. *Putting her clothes on display like that.*" He turns from the dress to look at me, his eyes narrowed.

Were we having a conversation?

"I mean, she couldn't even stand to be in the room with her visitors. She'd have conversations from another room," he says.

I imagine Emily Dickinson, from the next room, asking about things. *How's the weather, Claire? Is your life like a loaded gun?*

"It could be anybody's," I hear myself say quietly.

"Hmm?"

"It's probably not even her dress," I say.

"Of course it's hers. And she would have hated that it's there for people to see."

I shrug. "It's just a dress."

Mr. Tate is staring at me. He seems to have strong feelings about the dress. "Are you . . . still upset about that discussion?"

I feel my cheeks heat up. "Discussion?"

"The other day in class?"

It was that poem. I can still hear the real English teacher, Mr. Perzan, reciting it. I close my eyes and I can see his furry beard just slightly open as he speaks.

"Because I could not stop for Death—

He kindly stopped for me—"

"I don't know what you mean," I say. "Still upset about what?" On purpose I blink my eyes twice. Then I concentrate on the Plexiglas that separates us from Emily Dickinson's dress.

"I didn't mean to argue," he says, "about your comment. But most people . . ."

I hear myself let out some kind of sound—part laugh, part snort—when I hear him say "most people."

It must be something about the sound of the snort that stops him. I don't look over at him, but I can feel his eyes on me again, staring. Behind us, I hear the footsteps of large zoo animals, primates most likely—the type that like to stomp and drag their appendages, making their way down the stairs. They have found a reason to squeal over something I can only assume is highly amusing to primates.

Mr. Tate lets out a sigh.

"You mean, *most people*," I hear myself say, "don't think Emily Dickinson is funny? How is that even possible?" I do manage a voice that's sincere—like I'm really asking. I manage to overcome overt sarcasm. "Come on," I say, even sounding like I'm having a reasonable, friendly chat. "The girl in the poem is on a date with death. How is that not funny?" I make what I believe is a neutral gesture, one that indicates I am like *most people*. I watch my hand as it briefly glides through the air like someone else's hand.

"I guess if you're the *type of person* who thinks horror movies are funny," he says.

I feel the hair on my arms rise. I squeeze my lips together.

"I mean, the girl in the poem . . . she's cold . . . right?" he says.

He seems to have a compulsive need to convince me of something. "And she's being driven past a cemetery. She knows she's being led to her own end."

I continue to look straight ahead, to see nothing but the dress.

And then something—I'm not sure what—about the light outside shifts suddenly, like a curtain dropping over the sky, and the room is a new dim shade. Like it's a moment from a different, gray day.

"She wants to—" I hear my voice say. "She's making a decision to go with him. It's her choice."

"*What?*" He seems to whisper this. "What do you mean? Do you mean it's her choice to die?"

Does he step backwards as he asks this?

I swallow. I glance in his direction. He does seem farther away. I take a quick, sharp breath. I let out a fake laugh. It wouldn't convince anyone. "It's like a *cartoon*," I say. "That's what I meant the other day. *That kind* of funny. No big deal." I seem to be smiling, nodding, or I'm trying to anyway. I'm looking at him, or at least in his direction, but over his shoulder, out the window where things are blurred. My voice is even, so even it's flat. "Anyway, forget it. We just see the poem in different ways." Then I feel my feet start to move toward the door. I guess the rest of me follows. I don't know what happens to Tate.

"Why do you need to empty those boxes?" I ask. "It's better to have less clutter around." My father doesn't seem to hear me over the sound of his tearing tape off box tops. He is ripping dramatically, all arms and elbows. It's a violent sound that makes me shudder. For some reason, I think of skin.

As I watch him peeling back the top of the box, all the world's evil starts escaping and entering my bedroom. I can smell it.

I turn to my laptop. I type in *Flying Elvises* and shift the screen so he can't see it from where he stands as I'm lying on my bed.

"Everything's a mystery," my father says. "Why didn't we label the boxes when we packed? Now it's all a surprise."

"Surprises are bad," I say, but he doesn't hear; he's ripping another one open.

Yesterday, three Elvis impersonators died skydiving in high winds. It was meant to be a stunt to advertise the opening of a club in Springfield. If the Elvises have expressions on their faces in the video, you can't tell because of the effect of the wind on their cheeks. At first, they are showing off, arms and legs spread. One of them pretends he's swimming. I am thinking that's the worst part—the way they were having fun just before the end—and so I don't hear my father's question that ends in "cameraman, too?"

By now I see my father has managed to get a glimpse of my laptop as usual, in spite of the fact that it never makes him happy.

"Claire, must you?"

I turn to him. "It's a cultural artifact," I say. You'd think that as an archaeology professor he'd see that.

"It's macabre," he says.

"So many cultural artifacts are."

His mouth is in a grim, straight line. I see him wince as the screaming starts on the video, and I turn back quickly and press the MUTE button.

"How did school go today?"

"Average," I say. "Why do you need to empty the boxes anyway? All this stuff—it'll just get dusty."

"Average good?"

I'm not sure in which alternative universe *average* in regard to high school could be good. "Some interesting—uh—people," I say.

"You like it, then?"

I know it's a question, but it sounds more like begging.

I look at the screen. This is the part where things get confusing, where you can see the geometry of the town far below: inside the street grid you can make out twin baseball diamonds alongside a blue public pool.

So that's what you see when you fall to earth.

"We have enough stuff here already," I say. "We don't need the old things."

"Time to move in," he says, "and move on. We can't live in an empty house. I know it's not easy starting up someplace new in your senior year. But it's only a year. Think of it that way. Count down the days. Get through. That's all you have to do."

I hear him attack another box and its tape. He takes a deep breath, inhaling what's stored up in there. "Sylvia Plath. Anne Sexton. Randall Jarrell. Emily Dickinson," he says. "You're taking American lit, right? You might need—"

"I don't have room for those," I say, just barely looking up from my computer, where Springfield is silently flashing by, the blur accumulating.

I hear his feet shuffle. The sound echoes off the walls of this empty place.

"They were your mother's—"

"I know what they are." I switch to a new screen. "But I don't need them, Dad." My screen now has the picture of the nanny who was found yesterday in a dumpster in Boston—or rather, her torso was.

His feet do more shuffling. "Maybe we should do some exploring this weekend—get to know Amherst," he says. "What do you think?"

The nanny was Swedish and loved baking, I am reading. She had been dancing all night in a shiny silver top.

"The college has a great natural science museum," he says. "I can get us in after hours. We can have the place to ourselves." And just in case I didn't get the joke about his new job, he says, "I have connections there, you know."

In the *before* picture of the nanny, her white-blond hair is being whipped around her face by the wind at the beach. Of course, the children have been cropped out of the picture.

"It could be fun, just us and all those bones and rocks . . . Have you unpacked all of your clothes?" he asks.

I hear hangers sliding on the pole in my closet. Is my father really browsing through my wardrobe? I also wonder, *Where is the rest of the nanny? Where are her dancing feet?*

"Do you have some other clothes somewhere? Don't you have anything pink or yellow?" my father asks. I can hear the slow, deliberate movement of hangers against the metal pole as he examines my clothing, one item at a time. It's a chilling sound.

"You only said black was out," I say. "You didn't say anything about requiring pastels."

"You could use something bright. That was the problem in Providence, all that black."

This makes me laugh—that black clothes were my biggest

problem in Providence. "A guy broke our door down to get revenge," I say. "It didn't have anything to do with my clothes." I remembered the house shaking. Was I wearing black that day?

Another hanger slowly scrapes across the pole. *Note to self: Google* torso—*see if it means the head, too.*

"It was all related," he says.

"To my clothes?"

"This time we're going to do it right," he says. "You're going to finish high school. Did you see that catalog I found . . . J. Crew, I think. Does that sound right—J. Crew? I put it on your backpack." I hear him let out a deep breath. "You're going to move on," he says confidently. "Clothes are a start."

I look up at him. "A glass of water looks exactly like a glass of acid," I say.

He turns away from the clothes. "What?"

"Why does it matter what I look like?"

"You want this to work out, don't you?" It seems like a genuine question. Like a mystery even he can't seem to solve. "I'm just saying play along—get through the year. You didn't leave the house for months before we left Providence, and now you've been thrown right into things. Maybe you could use some help? I have the number of a doctor," he says. "Maybe some counseling—"

"Let me try," I say, "by myself."

He lets out a long breath.

"Can I try to work it out my way?"

Today Mr. Perzan, the real English teacher, is standing in the posture of a proud toy soldier. His suit, shirt, skin, and beard converge into the same shade of neutral. Only the textures distinguish clothing from person. It's easy to dwell on this coincidence of color in a classroom that's full of postlunch students, where the boys are sprawled out as if they are required to take up as much room as possible, like downed rain-forest trees, where the girls retract their elbows as you pass by. Like some rain-forest insects with a similar nature, even the most benign contact with them is taboo.

Mr. Perzan's tan beard opens. *"My life closed twice before its close."* The crystal-clear words lift into the air. He seems to have had some theater training, though those skills will be lost forever inside the rain forest. His past will die with him, here.

"What does Emily Dickinson mean—*My life closed twice?*" Mr. Perzan whispers to add intrigue.

Not one forest creature moves. The pretend teacher, Mr. Tate, is unfortunately seated facing AP English, at a student desk. Though he's trying awfully hard to imitate a real teacher in his shirt and tie, he fits right in to the forest, and seems to be dozing off. Perhaps the surfing championship did him in.

"Hmmm?" Mr. Perzan hums. "What does it mean?"

I feel my jaw tightening. I hear nothing except scratching, and see the girl next to me doodling in her notebook—a mob of garden gnomes with pitchforks, who all resemble Mr. Perzan.

"How does someone's life close twice before it really closes?" He's using another persona for this question—a skeptic. He leans back. He makes his shoulders droop. "It's not that whole death thing again. Is it?"

Still no response except the sound of pen on paper, etching in the details of many beards.

My eyes focus on the overly prepared football field outside, so bright green you couldn't help but notice it if you were falling to earth. It could be the last thing you'd see. I take a deep breath. This seems to make a lot of noise.

"It's not death," I am surprised to hear myself say. "It could be disappointment . . . or betrayal or something. You know, she's into the *drama* of it all. Saying that those things are like death." Did I wave my hand through the air, too?

The pretend teacher has awakened. Even from way across the room I can see signs of life.

"Drama?" Mr. Perzan asks. He lifts up his chin.

"Well, Emily Dickinson's life seems pretty boring," I say. As I speak, I hear the forest begin to stir. My cheeks get warm. I continue anyway. "It was a small orbit."

"A small what?" the pretend teacher asks from his corner. His voice is foggy from his nap. I can hear the forest creatures whispering.

"Orbit," I say quietly, and the room gets silent again. "I mean, her world was limited."

The pretend teacher is leaning forward, toward the forest. I watch his arm creeping toward the front of the desk. "Emily Dickinson's life was limited to mundane concerns? Is that what you mean?"

The forest eyes volley to Mr. Tate. You can hear the sound of tree trunks shifting, dragging themselves across the forest floor.

"I'm not saying feeling betrayed or disappointed is mundane," I say, "especially if you don't know much about life."

"You think they are on the same level as *death*?" Mr. Tate's voice gets high on the last word. The forest lets go of a single, collective murmur. The front legs of chairs lift and bang down.

"For some people," I say, though I don't know why I do. I hear the forest wakelings start to chirp. I close my eyes.

"And that Emily Dickinson didn't know much about life?" Mr. Tate is sitting very straight, his eyes very wide.

"I'll have to stop the discussion because we're out of time," Mr. Perzan says.

I only just now notice that he has moved off to the side and is leaning against the whiteboard, his arms folded.

"And, Claire," he starts, his voice sounding different again, more neutral and distant, "you should find out a bit more about that small orbit. See if it's true."

I finally find Emily Dickinson's grave in the cemetery at the center of town, tucked behind a strip of stores and near an apartment building. Her gravestone is surrounded by a wrought iron fence. It says "Born Dec. 10, 1830," and then it says "Called Back." It makes death seem so lifelike. Calling to her.

I am thinking of what that might sound like, when I hear his voice. It comes from behind me.

"Hi," he says. Mr. Tate, pretend teacher.

I glance at him. His face is red and sweaty, and his shirt's been labeled AMHERST COLLEGE, in case they misplace him. He's been running.

"Souvenir hunters still manage to climb inside to make rubbings of her gravestone," he says.

I turn back to the grave. "Makes sense." I mumble this.

"So you're really doing it?" he says. "Checking out that orbit?"

Even though I try to smile, I feel only half my mouth curl up.

"Why are *you* here?" My question comes out barbed. "Shouldn't you be at a fraternity party or something?" I ask, staring at his shirt.

His mouth smiles. I notice his eyes don't. "Shortcut. To my dorm— Oh, I get it," he says. He points to the little wooden box on the grave, where people have left things. I can see a note in a ziplock bag, for protection from the rain probably. "You're part of the club already, aren't you?"

His tone of voice cuts me. He's invaded my sector. *Lifeguard/ surfer, get back to your lookout post.*

I scowl at him and then turn to the tombstone. "What club?" I say.

"What's the measure of your grief?" he asks. I can't tell whether he's making fun of me or waiting for me to leap over the fence with some crayons and a paper bag so I can have my very own "Called Back" gravestone. He's watching my face to see if I got the reference.

I take a deep breath. I grip the fence tightly.

> *I measure every Grief I meet*
> *With narrow, probing Eyes—*
> *I wonder if It weighs like Mine—*

Ah, yes. *But none of those griefs ever do weigh like mine. It would be hard to do that.* I look straight ahead.

Lifeguard, shoo. Go home. "Fffff." Air leaves my mouth as I begin to deflate. I'm already tired of this town.

"It's okay to be in the club," he says, leaning on the fence. "It's not a sign of weakness." His voice seems to come from high above me, even though he's standing next to me. It has this way of coming down to my level.

I snort. "Lots of assumptions, Tate. You don't really know any-thing."

He starts to drop his wisdom on me. "I know what's obvious—"

"That I'm another emo high school girl?"

"Wait a—"

"*Very* perceptive," I say quickly, and turn to leave.

"Claire, I have some advice for you," he says.

I turn around to see his chin tucked down on his chest and his eyes looking at me from under the shelf of his eyebrows. If he wore glasses, he'd have them at the tip of his nose and he'd be looking over the rim. It's a look that says, "Listen up, I'm the head librarian."

Why don't I keep walking?

"Let me tell you something about senior year—"

I don't know if it's his tone of voice, so regulated and smooth—so *certain*—or the very idea that someone wants to tell me things about senior year, but a tiny rubber band in my head pops. I swear you could hear it *ping*. I feel the blood surge in my temples. "I already know plenty about senior year," I blurt out. My head throbs. "How many times did you do senior year, Tate? It's my *second time*—"

I stop suddenly and see his face now, the eyebrows lifting on his forehead. His head tilts.

I look at the gravestone. I imagine climbing over the fence and hiding behind it.

"Why? What happened?" he asks.

"What?" I close my eyes. I try to disappear, like a time traveler. There'd just be the slightest evidence of me then, a normal girl's sweatshirt and jeans left behind on the grass in front of Emily Dickinson's grave.

"Did you get sick?"

"Sick?"

"Why didn't you finish high school? Did you get mono or something?" His voice is matter-of-fact. He's even half smiling—doing me a favor, filing my life under Average, or at least somehow within the range of Usual.

"I—"

Why didn't you finish high school? It's a question I'm tired of answering, and I've been asked only once. This one time. *It was a rough couple of years,* I'll write in my college essay. *These people kept disappearing . . .*

I know it's possible I will be answering for the rest of my life if I don't get through this year, possible I'll have to tell the story over and over forever.

I stand up taller and grasp the metal fence bars. I hold on tight. How easy would it be for me to just say I had mono? *So easy.* Or to just say, "It's a long story." I look in his direction. But it's not him I see. Instead I see my old friend. Richy.

Richy.

It doesn't stop hurting, I could say, but I don't.

"I was a suspect in a missing-person case." I've never said it out loud before. It's like I'm auditioning for a play, forced to say someone else's dialogue—not the part I want—and it comes out naturally insincere.

And, believe it or not, that's just a small piece of the story.

"But . . . nobody can know," I say. "I just want to get through this year without it following me around."

Chapter 2

TATE IS NOT HALF SMILING ANYMORE.

He's standing very straight, his feet rooted against what looks like a blast of wind. Even his honey-colored curls seem to have been tossed back by the gale. I see his hands are making fists, like he's holding on tight to something. The rope that anchors him to normal maybe.

"I just want to finish something, and then move on to the next thing. To be almost not even here—practically invisible. You see?"

"Yeah," he says, his voice a bit muffled. "I see." He's battened down the hatches. He's deep inside there, under layers of something.

Well, that's *good*.

Just to make sure, I say, "I can't talk about it. You get that, right?"

He nods slowly, unconsciously. His eyes are very wide, very green and very liquid, and very much aimed at me despite how far away he seems now. I wonder what's going on behind them, but I quickly decide it's best not to know.

"Can you imagine anything worse than not getting out of high school?" I smile.

He doesn't smile back. He just keeps looking at me. "It's your story," he says. "I'm not going to be telling anyone."

September is taking longer than I expected it to. It seems to have days that replicate themselves in the same overcast way. The days have more than twenty-four hours in the same improbable way. I am finding it hard to get to sleep, and even if I do sleep, the spell expires at 2:30 a.m., just when the passing of time is suspended. I listen to the sounds of this foreign house, thinking a door is closing somewhere.

On one of these identical nights, I open up my laptop in my dark bedroom, so there is just the slightest blue, alien glow at my fingertips. My e-mail in-box is empty each time I do this. There is never an exception to this—it's mathematical, predictable, that I will not have a single message.

And equally predictable is that each night in suspended animation I will do the same thing. I will watch my slightly blue and alien fingertips type a message I delete a few minutes later. It always works the same—this act of futility—and this time the note says:

> *I knew that if we left*
> *I would never know*
> *when you came home.*
>
> (Are you home?)

I knew that if we left
I would not know
why you stayed away so long
                    (Why would you?)
and I would not know
where you had been all winter.
If you can, in your reply,
please state where.
                        (Every day it was cold I wondered
                        if you were warm.)
And then there are the same old questions
about that last night—
Why didn't you wait for me?
                    (I'M SORRY I was late.)
Why didn't I ~~remind tell~~ beg you NOT TO GO WITHOUT
    ME?
Why didn't I—IF NOT ME, THEN WHO WOULD?—tell
    you
                        (it's not the kind of thing that comes up in
                        everyday conversation)
it mattered whether you lived or died?

Out the window of the classroom it's morning, still September, and the electric-red trees seem to be the only bright spot in the gray picture. I experiment with blinking and seeing them projected on my eyelids.

Blinking is probably my first mistake. Keeping my eyes closed too long is my second. The crash of my calculator when it hits the ground wakes me. Everyone in the room turns first to look at me and then to watch the silver batteries of the calculator race each other to get under a desk. There will be no retrieving them with dignity, I know. And then, of course, I must consider whether I was snoring. I stare hard at the perfect squares of graph paper. But then I notice something. In my peripheral vision a calculator is bobbing just over my left shoulder.

I turn toward it slightly.

I let out a sigh. The girl behind me is smiling with enormous white teeth, in such a happy way it makes me think English is not her native tongue. And then I remember: She's the girl who was drawing the garden gnomes with pitchforks. And she's offering me her calculator.

"Uhhh. Thanks," I seem to say.

I watch her face lean closer to me. She says something that ends in "lunch."

She wants to have lunch with me?

"Why?" I ask. It's the first thing that comes to my mind. I open my mouth to say something else, but nothing comes out. I feel my eyes staring at the floor, at the place I last saw my calculator batteries before they vanished.

I hear her giggling quietly.

I glance back at her. She is one of those people who laughs with her whole face. Her eyes almost close up completely. She leans a bit closer and whispers, "I know. The cafeteria food is soooo bad."

"Oh." I take a deep breath and nod. "True, the food is bad, but it's the ambience I go for."

Another laugh overtakes her whole face.

"So, I'll meet you at sixth period?"

I watch her face, wondering if she's going to try to recruit me for a cult. Actually, I'd like to see the cult that would want me for a member. "O-kay," I say. "I'll—um—see you then."

On most nights at dinner, my father explains irrelevant things. Tonight he is lecturing about chemical imbalances, about how electrons and protons leave their assigned orbits, even though this is not his field of expertise. He manages to illustrate the concepts well, though, using his fork for emphasis. This evening's talk could be titled "Your Mother and Modern Pharmacology," except that when he talks about her, sometimes he says *a person*. "A person's chemical imbalance can overrule personality. A person's chemical imbalance can overrule logic," he says.

I still know who he's talking about.

I am thinking about a mutiny of electrons, what that might look like illustrated in a psychology textbook, each one a round ball with expressive eyebrows and a mouth that curves up only on one side. I am also thinking about what he doesn't say but wants to: A person's chemical imbalances can overrule love.

What he wants to say is: *It doesn't mean there was no love.*

"There was a bird," I say, "on the steps this morning. It was a baby bird. A dead baby—"

"What?"

"A dead bird on the steps this morning," I say. "I was wondering why."

I watch him place his fork on his plate so the tines curve downward. The gesture is careful, methodical. Final.

"Why what, Claire?" His voice is calm but edgy. Something about the dead bird obviously kills his craving for pork.

"I mean, it was probably a cat or something, but you have to wonder—*why?*" This is what I don't say: Where was its mother? Did she have a chemical imbalance, too?

"Wondering why?" He leans forward as he says this, closer to me, so close I can see the lines in his face, the way the edges of his lips curl downward. Tiny ropes could be anchored to them. Were they always like this?

"Oh, nothing—maybe it was bird flu or something—um— would it be okay if I didn't help with the dishes? I have a friend—"

"A friend?"

"Yes," I say. I pause. "And she's coming over."

"You have a friend coming over," he repeats, probably trying to convince himself that this could be true. He looks down at his plate. He's nodding silently. But then he stops. Without looking up he asks, "And did you tell her—?" He stops. His head is bowed toward the meat, as if he were giving thanks. I can see the fine strands of hair along the tippy top of his head, a mix of sand and gravel colors.

"I just met her," I say. And to make the point clearly, I add, "She *smiles* all the time."

He nods quickly. "Oh," he says. "I see." He picks up his fork and saws away mindlessly at his pork chop while looking at me. "What's your friend's name?" he asks.

"Tess," I say. "And she'll be here any minute."

I heard a Fly buzz—when I died. This is what Mr. Perzan wants us to think about. He's sitting on top of the teacher's desk, leaning forward as if he were about to dive into the pool of students.

"Imagine the last moment of your life—the moment before you see God or Krishna or your dead grandparents—and something gets in the way of that. Something distracts you." His hands chop at the air three times on the last words. "It's a really important moment—maybe *the* most important—and there's a fly buzzing . . ."

I close my eyes. I hear it.

"What would that mean to you?" he asks.

Though I'd rather not, I see my mother. I think about what she heard. The phone ringing.

And ringing and ringing and ringing. And then the whisper of her own last breath.

I hear myself take a deep breath, thinking about the phone call I tried to make, reminding myself I did that. I did call. And there she was: the moment she understands everything, and the phone rings.

A fly buzzes.

"It would be terrible," I say, so quietly no one hears.

Mr. Perzan writes on the whiteboard: "Write about an important moment. Recall the moment in detail. What did you see, taste, touch, and hear?"

Close your eyes. Taste first.

Juice on your lips. You open your mouth for more. Sour. Sweet. A taste that almost hurts.

Now look, she says. Blood oranges.

You are very small this first time.

She's laughing at your reaction, her laughs buoyed over the water in the river, on the rocks.

Blood oranges? You repeat. They sound evil. Are they a sin?

Laughter lapping at the edges. And the water and the stones.

It's the wrong color, you say.

Not for blood oranges, she says, her laughing voice surrounding you.

*It's a beautiful, beautiful color, she says, the words coming from all around
because of the water.*

*It is the color of light leaking from between fingers clasped over your
eyes, electric orange and red.*

*Sun flashes white on the creek, makes the edges of your irises curl and
hurt.*

*She's laughing, a continuous stream of that, like the creek water, she's
laughing and singing the silly rhyme—*

Claire, Claire, you walk on air—

"It's really beautiful," Tate says, looking over my shoulder. Tate
has a very sincere look on his face. "What happens—*or happened*—
next?" And something clipped on to the words. Fear?

"Next?" I try to swallow. My mouth has gone dry all of a
sudden.

"Yes, it's such a lovely, haunting moment, and the characters are
so clear. The little girl . . ."

A lovely haunting? *Is that what he said?*

Claire, Claire, you walk on air. Her voice and the sound of the
creek and the sky with its clouds . . .

"What happens," he asks carefully, "next?"

"Uh . . ." This is the part I have deleted, what happened next.

*The room was cold. You could barely remember the first part of the
day, the picnic, the water and light . . . the color of the oranges. This room
was dim and hushed. You knew how much things could change, even in
a single afternoon.*

*"She's not—dead," your father says. He's far across the room. This
is later that day. Her face is as white as the linens. "She's only sleeping,"
he says.*

He does not say she'll be okay.

You understand. He does not lie.

"Uh—you know, the day ends."

"But," he asks carefully, as if he's having a hard time with the next word, "how?"

Have some manners, Claire. The pretend teacher is making a very nice request. Tell him all the details of your mother's first attempt. How does this day end?

This time she wasn't called back, I could say. He'd get that.

"Average," I say. It really is the truth.

"I told you he'd like your story about the blood oranges," Tess says. We are sitting in the town common, under an enormous red tree.

"Hmmm? Who?"

"Who *else* is reading your stories? Oooooh . . . wait . . . *The student teacher, you mean? He* likes it?" She laughs and it sounds like bubbles. "That's even better."

I can feel my cheeks start to burn.

"Claire, you know that song—are we human or are we dancer?" Tess whispers, leaning close to me, her eyes laughing. Everything around Tess is buoyant. She has the ability to levitate things with her presence.

"Um, yes, I think so," I say. "Wasn't it voted the song with the dumbest lyrics one year?" As soon as I say this, I regret it. Why do I have to speak? Why can't I just laugh and nod?

But she laughs again. It's one of those laughs that seem to come from all over the place, that float. "Yeah," she says. "It's so random, right? Why not 'Are we leopard or are we exaggerated?'"

I laugh. It's been a while since someone's made me laugh so often. "Or 'Are we alien or are we swimming?'"

She laughs more. "Okay, let's play. Human or dancer?" She motions toward a girl walking by.

"Play?"

"That one—what's her story—human or dancer?"

A cool breeze blows through and a handful of bright leaves spirals down as a thin blonde walks by, huddled into herself, her arms clutching the strap of her enormous shoulder bag.

"Human," I say, "and in the movie about her, there would have to be an oboe playing in the background."

Tess nods. "Excellent point," she says. "The soundtrack is essential."

I take a deep breath. This is going okay.

"Do you believe in omens?" I ask, looking at the red leaf in my hand mostly, and Tess in peripheral vision. I believe I am holding my breath.

"Yes," she says. "Definitely."

I exhale. I continue. "The other day, when I left my house, there was this baby bird on the sidewalk." It had just a thin coating of something that might have turned into feathers eventually, and eyelids half closed over tiny, dull marbles. "Its skin was all wrinkly. Why is that? Why do young birds look like they're ancient?"

"I think it has something to do with reincarnation," she says.

I don't ask why she thought it might be right there, in my path to a new day, whether it was a bad omen. I hear Tess gurgle, and the ice in her cup rumbles. I remind myself this is a perfect autumn afternoon and that I am doing something ordinary—chatting with a friend on the Amherst common, where nothing (yet) has gone wrong. I notice my hand. I have mashed the radioactive-red leaf into a brown paste. I wipe the evidence off on my jeans.

"Oh, Claire, look, there's a yummy racial blend," Tess says, gesturing with her protein drink at a guy wearing shorts, defiant of the autumn chill. *"Dancer, absolutely."* The extralarge cup in her hands looks tiny, reminding me that Tess is gigantic—and perfectly proportioned. Until you stand next to her, you forget she's six feet tall. She could probably lift a car if she had to. Maybe she could handle what I might tell her.

"Uh, Tess . . ." I look very closely at the grass, trying to decide on another leaf to destroy. I concentrate on that selection. "You know my mother is gone and—"

She's looking at me.

"Sometimes I wonder if she's been, you know, reincarnated? Like I could be seeing her. Silly, huh?"

"No." She closes her eyes as she says this. "I'd wonder the same thing if I were you. Like, what do you think she would want to come back as—you know—if she had a choice?"

Ah. My eyes sting all of a sudden. "I—don't know." It's one of many things I wish I knew the answer to. "Maybe something with wings," I say.

"Wings?"

"She should get to fly this time," I say. "Maybe that would change things for her."

I look over at her then. She's looking at her empty cup. I've done that—made her look into emptiness.

"Hey," I say. "You're missing some excellent calves."

She looks up at the shorts guy and laughs. She leans back and stretches out, covering a great amount of grass. On cue, a flock of red leaves flutters down around her. "I'm pretty sure I could outrun him," Tess says.

"That would certainly make an impression on him," I say.

Step one: Determine the weight of a day's supply of dead birds.

"What's that?" My father is standing behind me, looking over my shoulder at my laptop, at the chart that tells you how to layer chickens with hay so that they'll compost. I hear him take a long sip of his overly filled coffee mug. I don't have to see it to know how full the mug is. The slurping seems endless.

"It's advice for a well-run poultry farm," I say.

"What?"

"I'm researching. For a project. For school."

"For chemistry?"

"For English," I say. "Poetry. I'm writing a poem."

> *Determine the weight of a day's*
> *supply of dead birds.*
> *Lift one.*
> *You can feel what's inside, you*
> *feel its nature: the wind.*
> *There's a reason they call it deadweight—*
> *you already know about the heaviness of dead things—*
> *but today lifting this one bird—all you can think about is air.*

I hear his footsteps. I hear the squeak of the kitchen chair as he sits. It squeaks again as he settles in. I hear him set his cup down.

I hear him sigh. I'd rather not see what he's doing with his face. Imagining is enough.

"Is your friend Tess writing poetry, too?" he asks. He emphasizes *your friend*, to remind me about the remarkable fact that I have one. The question itself is code, I know.

"Yes. It's a class assignment. Like I said."

Silence. Then the sound of slurping (this takes a while), pause, and the sound of the cup—clink—back on the table. It's a kind of ritualistic rhythm. Pause. I can expect him to speak right *now*.

"Is everyone writing poetry about composting chickens?"

I pretend I don't hear him. I smile, knowing he can't see my face. "Apparently," I say, "there is an ideal dead-birds-to-hay ratio."

"Claire." Pause. This is a long, silent pause. One that allows my imagination to roam.

"I've been meaning to ask you," he says, "about your college applications."

I lift my fingers off the keyboard.

His chair squeaks.

I move my hands to the edge of the desk.

"How are they . . . coming along?"

"I've been"—I wrap my arms around myself—"busy. With school."

Silence. Then one long squeak. "But you have your list from last year, right? It's just getting the old stuff out again."

Last year at this time, I was looking through brochures with Richy. We imagined our future in so many different ways. Our plans failed. Or something did. Luck, maybe. Or fate. I wish I knew which. "It seems wrong now," I say. I stare at the laptop screen, holding on to myself more tightly.

I hear the sound of his setting the coffee cup on the table. I don't have to see him to know how slowly he does this.

"You do want to go to college, don't you?" He almost whispers this.

"Sure—" I say. "Well . . . I think so. I'm just—" I pause. I turn to look at him.

His eyebrows are high on his forehead and his mouth is open. I'm surprised when I realize that he looks scared.

"What? What is it?" he says.

"It's just the old list . . . it was somebody else's list. I'm not the same. You know?"

I hear him exhale slowly. He lifts his cup but doesn't drink. "I could help you make up a new list," he says, and looks over at me. It's really more of a question, I know. "If you want. We could work on it together."

"Okay," I say. "We can try."

Chapter 3

THE DICKINSON HOUSE IS ALL DARK TONIGHT. I can hear my feet pressing over the dry leaves and fallen twigs. It's a sound that might give me away. I press my hand against the glass of the window and move my left eye close. I can see night-lights. It makes the house seem holy and haunted.

The window is open just a crack. I could get my fingers under that crack. I could get in there without anyone seeing.

I could.

The Jones Library is where I perform my community service, which, on college applications, will reveal my commitment to the world around me, but really all I'm asked to do here is make sure the alarm doesn't go off as someone tries to leave with a book. So I get a lot of homework done.

October seventh comes once each year . . .

I'm trying to focus on something other than the date, but I have to because the rain on the window sounds like pins, and because there was a circus at the Dickinson house today. When I walked by, on my way to the library, I saw a juggler in red-and-blue-striped pants. His face was painted white. The circus was meant to attract the attention of children to the poetry of Emily Dickinson—an effort to make it seem like something it's not.

The rain started gradually—thousands of pins on the yellow leaves—and he kept juggling as if he didn't care. You could hear the sounds of the knives sliding over each other clanging as they got wet, the clink as they met getting louder. You could see the black line around the juggler's mouth starting to blur. That kind of circus makes more sense at Emily Dickinson's house.

The rain is on the window now, alternating between soft and loud. I allow myself to type:

October seventh comes once each year.

I force myself to delete. I look at the window. All I see is blackness.

I type:

Some days are very significant: Anniversaries, for example, always appeal to terrorists. One day out of 365 is your birthday. And one of those 365 will be the day you die.

Again I press DELETE.

I found my mother on October seventh at six o'clock. Could I say she had been *called back*? Can you call yourself back?

I'll scare Mr. Perzan if I write that.

My father was on a late-afternoon flight that day, coming home from a conference where he had been delivering a paper on Pompeii.

He is an expert on big disasters, but only on what happens afterwards.

At the moment I saw her on the bed, he was probably seeing the blue lights of the runway. Or that's how I cut the film. I always add effects—when I see her, we hear the impact as the plane's landing gear hits the ground with a loud noise—speed and air and concrete.

I make this movie every October seventh.

After everyone had been called and the place emptied, my father and I would not leave our house, even though it was a place of terrible things. It was the only home we had on a night we truly needed one.

So.

I slept—or tried to fall asleep—in the same bedroom where I had slept for fourteen years. Out my window I could see a starless night and a fingernail moon. That part of it, the ordinariness after all the other parts, was nice to me.

In the morning, I woke up different for good.

I write about myself instead.

> *The last Night that She lived*
> *It was a Common Night*
> *Except the Dying—*
> *—Emily Dickinson*

Then she woke, remembering the sirens. The way they came from the air, like wind. The way they surrounded the house. The way they made her believe there was the possibility of rescue.

But there was no possibility, after all.

It was all just noise and lights.

And now it was morning. It could have been the next day or many years later. It was the same either way. The room seemed to inhale the pale light. For some reason she felt the need to stand. She shuffled to the dresser, but held on. There was a reflection in the mirror.

It was someone she could only slightly recognize. Her new self.

"Claire," Mr. Perzan says. "Another good piece." He talks to the papers in his hand, without looking up. "How much of it is fiction?"

"None of it," I say, packing up my bag. "It's my memoir." When I turn to leave, Mr. Perzan is gone, and Tate is standing behind me. Was he waiting?

"Memoir?" He says this quietly, almost in a whisper. "Is it that missing-person thing?"

I blink my eyes, hard. I can feel my jaw start to lock up. "You *said* it was my story." I look up at him. "You said I could keep it to myself."

He wrinkles his forehead. "I'm sorry. I couldn't stop thinking about what you said, and these things you're writing. I read that poem about the dead bird. These things you're writing about are—"

"Not really your business," I say. Such a short statement, but saying it still seems to take all my breath away.

He flinches, pinches his eyes closed as his chin moves upward in slow motion as if I've landed a punch.

It takes half a minute for his head to get straightened out, and when he starts to talk, he doesn't look at my face; he's looking at my hand, which, I also now notice, is gripping the back of a desk.

"Okay. Fair enough. Just be careful," he says. "Your work stands out. Your writing is—*dark*." He does look at me when he gets to the last word. He seems to be measuring my reaction to it, monitoring

my eyes for signs of trouble. He continues. "You said it was important to just finish the year, and you yourself said you want to be
practically invisible—*those were your exact words, right?* You want
to finish—"

"More than anything," I say. "I want to get past this." I nod. "I'm
sorry about what I said—about it not being your business."

He looks at me. He pauses. "Then just this—tell me—that
missing person. Did they—"

I hear laughter coming toward the door of the classroom. "No,"
I say quickly. "That's not what this is about. This one is about my
mother. She's not missing," I say. "She's gone for good."

I'm at the Amazing Bean. *You'd better start swimming or you'll sink
like a stone,* Bob Dylan is singing. I am looking at sad Tess. Her
throwing is off, and it's her specialty. She's going to an indoor track-
and-field meet this weekend where she might hear confirmation
that she's stopped improving. For a while, every time she threw
something, it went farther—the discus, the shot put, the javelin.
She got used to being a superhero in training.

Now that she's earthly, she's stopped looking at boys.

"Human or dancer?" I ask, gesturing with my face to a boy in a
bright green shirt at the table across the shop. I hate that she doesn't
even look.

"Leopard or exaggerated?" I smile.

No response.

"Did I infect you?" I ask.

She looks up, her head a very heavy, large thing that is a burden
on her neck.

"I usually just make sad people sadder," I say. "I don't have much experience with you of the cheerful persuasion. Have I contaminated you, too?"

"No, not you. You make me laugh, Claire."

I stare at her in disbelief. *What did she just say? That I make her laugh?*

Her face is a billboard, stripped clear, obviously blank. She has nothing. I haven't been in the position of having to be someone's flotation device—honestly, it never comes up anymore—so what I should do isn't immediately clear.

"I've stopped growing," she says. "I won't ever get any taller."

"That's what's bothering you?" I feel myself squinting at her. *That's a problem?* Well, it's *my friend's* problem. I try to relax my face. I nod. "I've been five foot three since I was fourteen," I say. "I'm so average, I'm invisible."

"Invisible—are you crazy? You have that thing you do when you talk. People can't wait to hear what you're going to say next. Even that student teacher pays attention, and everything seems to bore him."

"Whhhat? You are *delusional*. People just think I'm weird. I'd be better off invisible." I pull my arms out of my jacket for something to do so she won't notice how red my face is.

She shakes her head. "That's why I like you. You aren't afraid to say what you think. I'm so tired of all the pretending."

"Well, you, Tess—you are strong and beautiful and you have perfect teeth," I tell her. She looks at me, still slightly hopeless but willing to listen. Maybe a little bit more than willing.

"Did you ever feel like you stopped getting better?" she says. "Like one day your life just flattened out and you might never get any better at anything?" Her eyes are glossy. "Like you lost your chance?"

I lost a whole year, Tess, I want to say, to make somebody understand what that felt like. A whole year of my life was put into a box and sealed up, and I don't know whether more will get sucked into that box, too.

"Ebbs and flows," I say instead of all that. "My mother used to say we're mostly water. That it's natural for things to come and go. The ebbing happened, and now it's time for some flow—right? I see something new on the horizon, something unexpected. A very tall, very dark stranger—half human and half dancer—a rare breed, just your type."

I hear her chuckle. "That *would* be my type." She smiles, and because of that, I do, too.

Chapter 4

A BOY IS MISSING. A boy is missing. A boy is missing. It flashes on the bottom of television screens, stopping the year from moving forward.

Please look for him, they say.

He is from the next town over, Hadley. People aren't usually missing from Hadley, and everyone is looking for him, lined up elbow to elbow. You see pictures of him everywhere.

I never met this boy, but boys go missing. You don't want them to, but they do. They go missing and weeks get lost, then months.

"Claire." It's Tate. "I've been trying to catch up with you since last week."

"And now you have," I say.

"Claire?"

I'm standing near the glass window and feel the cold of it, radiating inward toward this classroom that still smells like soap and leather even though the students are gone.

"I'm not trying to pry . . ." Tate's voice sounds like seagulls. It's English, but not the kind I speak. He seems to want something.

I look out the window. Fog has overtaken the football field. It's damp and gray, and another boy is missing, and the year is slowing down. Instead of this boy in Hadley, I'm thinking of Richy.

"Claire, do you hear me?"

Tate's standing beside me. He must not be able to see how tired this missing boy makes me, how I could sleep in the blurry woods for a hundred years, become ashy there, and later windswept.

"If your mother wasn't the missing person, then . . . ?" he asks.

A boy is missing, Tate.

He was last seen.

Searchers line up elbow to elbow in the woods by the Quabbin Reservoir, looking for pieces of cloth, hair, teeth. His parents say *Please. Please. Please.* Even after I press the MUTE button I can read their lips.

I know what they mean.

I want to help, but I wouldn't know a bone fragment even if I saw one. "I'm too tired," I try. Not only has time stopped, but the past seems to be rewinding.

Back to the other boy. He went missing nine months ago.

Richy.

Tate maintains the tilty, intense stare.

"I'm too tired for sharing time." I look out the window. I breathe in the scent of my classmates deeply.

Tate's voice is birdy. It reminds me that seagulls beg like people, in people voices. Or is it the other way around? *Mo-ore. Mo-ore.*

His seagull voice is near my ear. The humanity in his seagull voice makes me look for something because he seems to want me to do that. To see something out the window.

"A cardinal," he says about a red bird that flies past our reflections and into the fog. I hear him sigh.

Birds and birds and birds and birds . . . I think I might say.

Window, fog, football field.

Golden dog on the ten-yard line, emerging from the mist.

I stop breathing. On the football field the golden dog is carrying something in his mouth.

I gasp. "The dog's got the cardinal."

"Claire," he says. He sounds like a person now, with a calm late-night radio voice. He's all I hear. "It's a Frisbee. The dog's just playing."

The dog is romping, fading in and out of the fog. Like always, someone I can't see is on the other end of the field, pulling the strings.

"Claire, are you all right?"

"The missing person—not the one here, the other one, the one in Providence—he was my best friend, Richy. He still hasn't come home."

He looks at me. It seems like he's confused.

"The last time I saw him was February. I was the last one to see him, the last one he called—" I find myself rambling. "After a while, they decided I didn't know where he was. Because I didn't. I don't."

I stop and look at the fog, the way it erases things you're sure of. It makes me feel lost. I look back at Tate, but he's not looking at me anymore. "You believe me," I ask, "don't you?"

* * *

How to start with Tess? The last time I saw Richy . . .

It was real winter, Tess, I might say. Ducks were swimming in a small thaw in the ice stream behind the mall. The runoff water was a toxic shade of orange, as usual. The ducks were surrounded by ice that looked like broken glass. It was a dangerous-looking picture, the drab birds and the glass shards. Richy had just emptied a whole box of Tic-Tacs into the water. The ducks dived among the broken ice and into the water, quacking and arguing before pointing their behinds skyward.

"You've driven them to cannibalism," I said.

"I have that effect on wildlife," Richy said.

He was—is—funny, I could say to Tess. He is really a funny kid. A really sad and funny kid.

It was cold—too cold for the light leather jacket he wore, and for his bare hands.

"So," I say. "What's been going on?" I haven't seen her for a while.

"Willis Franklin has been going on. He's something like six foot eleven," she says, smoothing down her electric waves of hair. Her fingernails are painted a tropical color that looks even more spicy in her dark hair. Just the idea of him makes her hair stand on edge. "He's complicated." She makes this sound like a good thing.

"Then I was right about the tall, dark stranger. It was Frankly Franklin and he's complicated." I nod.

"That's right. You're *Claire Voyant.*"

I think about my mother and I think about Richy.

Tess, if I knew what came next . . . I want to say. *If I knew, then I could have stopped them. I would have stopped them.*

I would have.

"I had a best friend named Richy," I say. "He was complicated."

"Was?"

"Yeah, he's . . . well, I lost him . . ." I try to say more about that, but I can't. Instead I ask, "But this Frankly Franklin—he's definitely a dancer?"

"I think there's some dancer potential, yes," she says, her eyes rolling.

"Dancer *and* human?" I ask.

"Let's not overrate the new stock yet," she says. "We don't want to undervalue those rare hybrids, now, do we?"

"Who knows about tarot?" Mr. Perzan asks. I'm late for class. I trek through the disaster forest full of downed tree limbs and slide into my seat.

Mr. Perzan reaches into his pocket and pulls out a card. He throws the card, and at first a forest wakeling is pleased to have caught it. The boy holds it aloft, so others might worship. The boy nods in an exaggerated, self-congratulatory way, raising the obligatory fist bump to the sky.

But then, the wakeling shouts, "Death?!" and flings the card like a hot potato. *"Why'd you give me Death?"*

Mr. Perzan nods knowingly. He strokes his pet beard and crosses his corduroy arms over his chest. I suspect he's done all this before.

"What did Death look like?" Mr. Perzan asks the boy who threw it. "Did you notice he was riding a horse? Death is traveling, moving, changing."

Oooh . . . A murmur begins: the forest is interested now.

"Death is the thirteenth card in the deck. The thirteenth card really has nothing to do with dying, physically," Mr. Perzan says.

"It's about transition, change—about saying goodbye to one thing and moving on to the next. But that's a kind of death, too, right?" He picks up his book and starts to read. *"A Light exists in Spring . . . It waits upon the Lawn."* He stops and looks over our heads, and then I hear my name. "Claire."

I swallow. *Why involve me in your theatrics?*

"Claire, is Emily Dickinson optimistic in this poem?"

"No," I say quickly. "Nothing good is ever waiting on your lawn." I can say this from experience. Even though I probably shouldn't say it out loud.

The forest erupts in cheers.

This is certainly not what I'd intended.

I look at Tess, who is squeezing her eyes shut tightly.

Mr. Perzan nods, holds up his hand, and continues. "How about death in her poems? Can death be like the thirteenth card? Not really about dying per se, but *changing*?"

"After great pain, a formal feeling comes . . ." I read from her poem. *"This is the Hour of Lead? . . . First—Chill—then Stupor—then the letting go—?* Sometimes dying is really dying."

Mr. Perzan's hands go to his hips. He's in the posture of a soldier. From a body-language perspective, I'd say it's a bad development. Inside, I'm cringing. Outside, not so much.

"Okay, then, sometimes she means it—*as Claire points out*—and sometimes she doesn't," he says. He turns to the whiteboard. "Emily Dickinson, *like everyone else in the world*, had more than one thing to say. Prove that to me in your next paper." He writes, *For Monday.*

The forest groans. The trees take it out on me in hisses and sideways glances.

* * *

"You found them again?" my father asks. He finds me lying on my bed surrounded by the books.

"I was just looking for the Dickinson book, but I found all the rest of these. It's for—homework." I open my eyes. He is leaning against the door frame.

"It's been a while since anyone read them . . ." His voice is soft. He's looking around the bed.

"I forgot she had all this poetry." I reach out without looking at them and pat the books as if they were small pets.

"She'd had them for a long time—her whole life . . ." His voice trails off.

I can see the dust motes in the bands of sun through the window. The dust from the books makes my eyes sting.

When he starts to speak again, it sounds far away. "You changed your mind? You didn't seem to want to—"

"I didn't—*don't*. It's for this assignment, like I said," I tell him, looking at the ceiling. "I'll put them back into the boxes right after I finish this paper. *I will*." I fold my hands over my heart like a corpse. I hear him turn to leave.

"You don't . . . have to." I think this is what he says. It's a whisper.

"Dad—"

He turns back, and I look over at him.

"Am I crazy or do you smell that, too?" I ask him.

"The old house, right?"

"That's what *I* was thinking," I say.

It's oregano. And pine. Oh—and lavender. That kind of French soap he brought home for her whenever he traveled. I could say,

That's what we smell—the floors that looked like honey in the sun, the things she was always cooking in massive pots, the soap you always brought.

But I don't.

"These books. They're carriers." I hear him sigh.

"Yeah," I say. "Seems like that."

When he leaves, I take out my notebook:

> *How is a box of books like a wound? is the question.*
> *The sound the tape/bandage makes when you*
> *rip it off the surface is one way, one answer to the question.*
> *Another one is finding a book and seeing that your mother*
> *(a long time before you were born)*
> *underlined a Dylan Thomas poem—*
> > *Time held me green and dying*
> > *Though I sang like the sea in my chains.*
> *And the way her notes in the margins, like stitches,*
> *show you all the places where she felt*
> *the insistent and jagged*
> *little cuts of each new day.*

The first time the girl breaks into Emily Dickinson's house there is no moon.

A window, I have noticed, is always open a crack, even in November. I slide my fingertips along the bottom, feeling for trip wires, and gradually pull just a little. The window resists, but gives.

I lift my leg over the edge and slip into Emily Dickinson's house. My heart beats wildly. I am experiencing what the worshippers do when they come to this place, but my rush is ten times better. I lower the window. There are a few small night-lights along the walls, filling the house with long shadows and the almost-lost scents of an empty house. There is ginger under there and maybe maple, the edge of eucalyptus from when the children caught colds. This house remembers Emily Dickinson. I close my eyes and hear her breathing.

When I open my eyes this is what I see: Emily Dickinson's dress. It's hard to believe it's hers, but I'm starting to. And with this light, just a small glow of night-lights around the perimeter of the room, this does seem like a holy place. A place where more than one lost soul might be.

I listen to them, breathing.

I find an empty page in my notebook.

"I felt my life with both my hands," Emily Dickinson said,
"To see if it was there."
I want to write I know what she means.
I wake up in the middle of the night,
the way you might, wondering where you are.
I smell the air and know everything
has changed—chalk and tea
are in this air, the smells of a fire
someone lit last winter.
It wasn't our fire is what I remember, that
my father and I were elsewhere, and cold all last year.
I wake up and touch my face, to see if I am here.
I say, This is Amherst, my room.
I say, You live here, now. I tell myself,

Your father is just down the hall. And because I forget
and have to remind myself, I say, Your mother
is gone. And it was her choice,
a decision she made.
Even though it's been a while,
sometimes when I am outside and there is wind
through the leaves I think I hear her
breathing, or turning the pages
of a book in an empty room—
This is what I do: I look up, hoping
to see her, even if it's one last time. I reach out
so I can feel her life with both hands.
But nothing's there.

The year's first snowfall always seems like the world's first.

I am waiting for class to start, sitting at a desk that looks out on a field with fresh snow, a fill-in-the-blank sort of viewpoint. A woman is walking on that white page, followed by her footprints. *Exit, pursued by a bear.* An invisible bear.

My laptop is open to the only picture of Emily Dickinson ever taken. She was seventeen in the picture. She will be seventeen forever because of the picture.

"How did you do with that paper? Does Emily Dickinson have more than one thing to say? Something optimistic, maybe?" A representative of the Amherst College rowing team has officially entered the room. You can tell who he is from his fine purple jacket.

All, please rise.

I close my laptop quickly.

"Wait, don't tell me. You started with *I dwell in Possibility—*"

I hear the smirk in his words. I look over at him—the way he seems amused by everything. *Is it wonderful to be you, Tate?*

"Emily Dickinson had her own way of looking at the world. It just wasn't like everybody else's. She was alone in that way," I say. I also don't say: *She was like my mother.* I'm starting to see how much.

"What makes you think she was alone?" Tate asks. He sits at a desk—I notice he makes sure not to remove the jacket—and leans way back.

Because I'm having conversations with her, I could say, *at night, IN HER HOUSE*—and watch the expression on his face. That might be interesting.

"People wanted her to be somebody else. They tried to change her. Her father tried. You've read the same stuff I have. About how he wanted her to be more devoted to God. How he took her to the revival meeting and it went badly."

He's making a steeple with his fingertips. He's looking at the steeple. I hear the chatter of students behind me, entering the classroom.

"Her father led her by the hand into the tent. They all gathered around her. They wanted her to profess her faith, but she said no. Can you imagine it?" I look him in the eye to make sure he's really listening. "This tiny young woman saying 'No.' Maybe it was very dramatic—as she rose to leave, maybe, her wooden chair fell backward. Maybe it crashed to the ground. Maybe she didn't even recognize her own voice as she said no. 'NO.'" I can feel how wide open my eyes are.

"So she said no to what?"

"She said you can't force me to believe something I don't. You can't force someone to have faith," I say, and because it's on my mind, I also say, "or hope. Either they do or they don't have it."

I think about my mother again.

I look over at Tate. I've forgotten what this conversation started out as. He seems to have the same problem. He's lost somewhere else, methodically taking apart the church. "Eh, how are your college applications going, Claire?"

I shrug.

And then his librarian voice gets flicked on: "You're going to have a life after high school. You'll finish this time and you'll move on. You know that, right?" He's leaning back while he talks, in that way jocks usually do.

"How can you be so sure of *everything*?" I ask. "On which planet is everything so reliable, and how long does it take to get *here* on your spaceship?"

He looks up. He's still got that wrinkle and the church is all gone.

I hear desks moving as students fill up the room and Mr. Perzan takes his place up front. I lower my voice but look directly into Tate's eyes so he gets what I'm saying. "The fact is, you don't know who's going to have a life and who's not," I say. "You don't know who's going to stop at seventeen. I don't, and neither do you."

Chapter 5

HOW TO RECOVER AFTER TRAUMA:

1. Understand that your feelings are normal.
2. Remember that the pain does not last forever.
3. Take good care of yourself.
4. Listen to yourself.

My father is up to some new tricks. He leaves this list, printed out from a website, on my desk. Though I am intrigued about an Internet site that might count me in the category "normal," I am tempted to crumple up the paper and put it in the trash. For some reason, I do not.

Is it his way of saying, *You need to have a life, Claire*? Or is it one of those things you tell others when you're really trying to convince yourself of the same thing?

It's become unnecessary to tell Tess about my *past* since Frankly Franklin came into the picture. I have been wondering how it might have turned out—having a friend. I have been feeling regretful and relieved at the same time. I know from experience that losing her now is better than losing her later. But then, today Tess slams herself into the wall. It's December in Massachusetts, so she's loosely covered in an array of winter layers, all dangling. As she hits the wall, the scarves and coats and sweaters sway. The impact makes the sound of a dictionary dropping.

The Romance is over.

Her lips are cracked and chapped, and her face is terrible—still raw with the panic of disappointment. This should never, ever happen to Happy Tess.

Even *my* heart hurts.

I wish this came with a manual, like trauma does.

HOW TO RECOVER AFTER LOVE:

1. Understand that your feelings are normal.
2. Remember that love does not last forever.
3. Take good care of yourself.
4. Listen to yourself.

"You need a carnival," I say. "There's a holiday fair on the common. Tents and crafts and stuff."

Her whole face loosens up. Her eyes are starting to smile. That she is as resilient as a rubber band makes my day.

It's good for Tess that the crafts tent is full of wonder. This will occupy her. The whole afternoon we can watch wet clay spinning on wheels and origami mobiles and room-sized looms.

Tate is here, wearing a blazer, wandering around with a matching blonde who has very large boots. Every once in a while, I see the blonde pick up something. Tate responds to it by making that exaggerated pantomime face Spanish teachers like to use when they're compensating for their students' lack of vocabulary. The blonde cracks up, holding her belly. Her sides might split.

It's remotely interesting to me that in Tate's life people are laughing. It's not surprising that they are laughing. It's common enough for that to happen.

I understand I probably shouldn't be watching them laugh.

The same excessive humor is among some skeletons who are grinning hysterically on one of the craft tables. They are small figures, carved and painted. Some play in a rock band. One rides a bike. The sign reads: "The Día de los Muertos figures remind us that the dead love us! They want to be part of our lives!" I buy the punk one with the Mohawk for Tess, an early Christmas present.

When I notice Tate and his friend heading over to the table, I duck.

By the time Tess finds me, her cheeks are rosy again. She's back in action. "The glassblowers are over there," she says, naturally drawn to three large men who, among the crafters, seem like Olympians. They have long pipes that end in large bubbles in pretty colors.

Tess elbows a path close to the platform where they work.

Though the amount of breath they seem required to hold in their cheeks seems life-threatening, they put on a good show. The young one has a face that looks like a charcoal sketch, particularly his thick eyebrows. They arch as he makes jokes about when not to inhale. The university women with handwoven scarves and dangling earrings laugh and laugh. He is, you can tell, used to fooling around with the concept that older women love a craftsman.

After he puts his cobalt ball flecked with little spots of cadmium yellow in its cooling bath, Tess gasps. "I've never seen a color like that. Never."

This is why Tess must always be my friend: the glass has taken her breath away.

He has heard her. His whole face smiles. You can see what's in his head, how important the color is, and how he is glad someone loves it. I watch him: he has forearms like Popeye, and a big barrel chest. Tess doesn't notice at first, but he's looking at her—his illustrated eyebrows and everything. He won't take his eyes off her.

He's still working, rotating the glass in the water, but his eyes are on her. I look at her, too. When she looks at his face and realizes he's looking at her, she blushes.

I think I hear something. Does the door in the heart make a noise when it opens?

I find a list at the glassblowers' booth. I take a copy. When I get home I'll highlight the last line before I drop it off on my father's desk—another example of advice you give others and yourself at the same time.

SAFETY PROCEDURES FOR GLASSBLOWERS:

- Keep your work area tidy. The potential for cuts and burns is highest when the work area is cluttered with unnecessary materials.

- Avoid distractions: stay focused on your glassblowing bench, particularly if you are working near others.
- Know the location of exits.
- Know how to shut off the gas.
- **<u>Most important: Do not work alone</u>**—<u>be sure someone is always close by.</u>

Chapter 6

WE'VE STARTED ON HAMLET, who can't get past himself. It's obvious the real tragedy is Ophelia, but nobody sees that because she's in the margins, pressing flowers in books.

Tess says she's like Ophelia, on the sidelines, waiting around, because Gus the glassblower is always busy with craft shows now, and after Christmas he'll be heading back to boarding school in Vermont.

Live in the moment, I could say, with a manufactured Zen kind of cheerfulness. *Live for today.*

"It's not the way I thought it would be," she said. "You're supposed to be the star when you're the leading lady, aren't you? You're supposed to be in demand."

We are early for class, waiting for Perzan to march into the room, followed by the forest wakelings. Some of them are wrestling tonight. They have been rehearsing on the stairway landings and open spaces in the cafeteria, causing some collateral damage, making the school seem like Sparta.

"I don't even know if I am the leading lady," she says.

She wants somebody to tell her that she and Gus are going to last forever. That there are obstacles, but sure, it gets better. A good friend would do that. Any other friend except me. I can't seem to say things I don't believe.

I could say this: *Tess, realistically, some things—even with the best intentions—never go well.* That's something I believe.

I think for a second. "You know those princess dresses with all that stiff netting under the skirt? All little girls want one?"

She shakes her head. "I wanted a motorized jeep."

"Okay, but say you wanted one of those really poufy princess dresses with all that scratchy stuff. And you put it on and you felt like somebody from a fairy tale, but then you noticed how painful that net was, how itchy and awful, and you said, 'This is horrible. This dress hurts. Mommy, why didn't you tell me?'"

"Yeah?"

"And what would she say?" I ask.

"She'd say, 'But that's what you asked for.'"

"My mom didn't," I say. "She said, 'You have to figure out if it's worth it.'"

She looks down, at the floor, and then she looks at me. "Your mom said that?"

I nod. "Exactly that."

She looks back down again. The room is filling up with kids trying to capture each other while the others run for cover, so I can barely hear her, but Tess doesn't have to say this loudly for me to know she really, really means it.

"It's worth it."

* * *

There has been some kind of celebration at the Dickinson house—it's close to her birthday, I know, and for the past week, the lights of the house have been on way into the night. My father has been extra distracted with a project about Egypt involving another professor, and if I could get in there, I could stay late.

I am dying to get in there and work on my story. *Dying.*

It's Friday, and the college students are all polished up for a Friday night, the girls in sweaters and suede boots. A group of them leave the coffee shop armed with enough frozen caffeine drinks to keep them up until Sunday. The students seem to be always laughing. As they leave, the wind through the door carries the scent of their trail—candy, lilacs, strawberries.

I look at my watch. I can make my first attempt in forty-five minutes when I'm sure everybody's gone. Sigh. It's a long time to watch happy people make entrances and exits.

I take out my notebook.

Reading Emily Dickinson by Flashlight with My Mom

Who explained that pollen looks like
cheese powder from Doritos.

"Claire?"

Uh-oh. *Don't look up.*

"Claire."

Deep breath. Close the notebook.

I look up at Tate. He's wearing a gray sweatshirt (guess what's written on it?), and his hair is wet, stuck to his face. He's all sweaty.

"Yes?"

"Hey, Claire—" He wipes a line of sweat off his forehead. His face is red, making his green eyes more apparent. "I was running by and noticed you in the window. I saw you at the craft show last week. When I walked over, you turned and walked in the other direction. Did I do something wrong?"

I swallow. My mouth is very dry, and my mind a blank slate.

"I didn't see—I mean, *I saw you* but didn't *see* you—I mean, I wasn't *watching*"—I clear my throat—"you." There is certainly no hiding the redness of my face, so I won't even bother to try. "I was neither avoiding nor not avoiding you," I say. "I was being . . . neutral on avoidance."

He looks puzzled.

"I hate," I say then nonchalantly, "Hamlet." I can manage a calm voice. "Not the play—the person." As far as distractions go, it's not a good one.

His hand is on his hip and I'm slightly turned to look at him. He's standing, and at any moment droplets of his sweat are going to hit me from up there. *From inside that tower up there with you looking out the window.*

Plip. One drop hits my journal. *Plip.*

Tate is sweating on my notebook instead of talking. His eyebrows are doing that arching thing, that high-expectations-in-the-middle-of-the-coffee-shop thing.

"You're okay?" he asks.

"Okay?"

"You seem a little—" He blinks blankly. His voice is so extra calm it's scary. "Edgy."

"Hmmm?"

"Last week, that thing you said—"

"Last week?" I'm trying to remember—I really am.

"Claire, do you need help?" he says, suddenly changing tone. It seems urgent that he know the answer.

"Help?" Now I'm confused. *Help with getting coffee?*

He glances down at my notebook. "What you said about who won't be getting past seventeen?"

Plip. I stare hard at my notebook, where the dark sweat stains expand like the influence of an occupying force on a small, sheltered country. That's when it starts clicking in my head that he's been reading my writing—all of it. Absorbing it.

And I've told him my backstory. He has both halves. He has them because I've given them to him. I *gave* him this power over me. *Why?*

"Mr. Perzan and I—"

The rest of this happens quickly and slowly at the same time, like time-lapse photography: me suddenly figuring the whole thing out. "YOU TOLD PERZAN?"

I can hardly find the air, but next I'm saying, in a small voice, much smaller than you would expect, "You told him *my story?*"

Then I hear myself make some kind of noise.

"I was worried, but—" he starts.

Though things seem to be moving at high speed, I manage to make that sound again. It's like a laugh, but it has no humor. It comes from deep inside my throat, the way a villain's laugh would. It *does* sound crazy.

I'm standing up and, at the same time, reaching in two directions, sweeping up my coat and bag and pen and mittens and notebook—my heart pounding so loudly you can hear it. It's not a *good* sound. "I'm not *anybody's* project. Not Perzan's," I say. I can feel a second dose of heat injecting itself through my cheeks and up to the top of my ears, maybe even my scalp. *"Certainly not YOURS."* Then the chair tips and Tate catches it and my journal falls and opens. I bend down to get it and a crowd of college students is trying to enter and everybody is crowded against everybody else, nudging to get out. To get away.

My face burning hot.

The door opening with that sound. It's like the bell in a boxing match.

Did I just run away from Tate?

Real smooth, Claire. *Real smooth.*

I press the sides of my head hard. I want to squeeze out what keeps replaying on the loop in there: This is Providence all over—people are making decisions about me. Watching me. And I have to run away again—I am on the street, where everyone has someplace to go, in zigzag patterns, and they are going to those places, and I am walking in circles, hearing buzzing.

Every once in a while I stop to rub my eyes. I'll get used to the dark soon.

I find the trash can and stash my backpack behind it. It's easier to climb through the window without it.

I find the gap in the window. Nobody sees this but me.

I lift it. I climb over the sill.

The smell of snow on the winter air fades. I take a deep breath. I smell paper. Here I have the cool, clean feeling of paper, too.

I am so glad to get away. To be in Emily Dickinson's house.

I close my eyes, and remember.

Reading Emily Dickinson by Flashlight with My Mom

Who explained that pollen looks like
cheese powder from Doritos.
Who explained that magic dust
is inside every single flower—
So, basically, magic is everywhere.
Who said, I'll read you <u>one</u> more,
and QUICK, LOOK—
the moon has climbed
over the neighbors' rooftop
and is sitting on their chimney—
Just try to tell me you see THAT every day.
Read the one about the mermaids in the basement?
Good choice, she said, holding the flashlight
while I turned the pages of Emily Dickinson.
That's when magic was still living
in all the houses and was ordinary as a whole sky
filled up with stars.

"Claire!"

I open my eyes. I hear my name in a terrified voice. I hear a noise—high-pitched like a machine.

"Claire, do you hear me?" It's dark. Somebody has my elbows. He is shaking me as if to wake me up. I'm not asleep, though I am in the dark.

"Wh-what?"

"Don't you hear the alarm?"

It's Tate's voice in the dark. In Emily Dickinson's house? Tate's voice? I hear something buzzing. It's so dark that I don't see him. I see the shape of him, standing close to me, his hands on my shoulders. Shaking me.

"That's an alarm?" I ask. "I don't think—"

"Claire, we don't have time to talk about this." His voice has the urgency of Niagara Falls in my ear. That's when I feel his hand grip my elbow tightly, so tightly it hurts. It's like I'm stuck on the fender of a truck and being pulled, dragged.

Hurry. I hear fumbling, the back door opening. Moonlight. The ground is under my feet. Our bodies cut through the bushes and there's a siren far off, winding and unwinding. Branches on my face.

I feel Tate's arm around me. "Through there—fast," he says, pointing to a place where a fence seems to have a gap between boards, and between the boards there is blackness.

"I can't—the dress—" But he has one arm around my waist and the other over my head, hugging me so we can both get through the small opening.

RRrrip.

"Oh no," I call out.

"Shhhhhhhh," he hisses, tugging at the top of my arm. He pushes me forward, his hand clutching my arm. I can hear our movement through the branches. A dog starts barking. We are near a shed in a backyard. The dog is in the house. Breathing, catching my breath, gulping for air.

My lungs burn but I am afraid to stop my feet. The way the

moon stutters through the bare branches, like the flickering of an ancient movie.

We are changing direction, turning into a clearing. I start to recognize where we are now. We must have come through the backyards and made it to the cemetery where Emily is buried. We are under the hemlocks. I am doubled over, trying to catch my breath. I might throw up.

"I don't hear anyone behind—" I start, but I stop because when I look up, I see Tate, in the moonlight.

His eyes are wide, and he seems to have stopped breathing altogether.

"That's not—my God, Claire. I can't believe you're wearing that dress."

Chapter 7

IT'S TRUE. IN THE DIM LIGHT of the moon through all those branches, Emily Dickinson's dress is a ghostly relic. It's hard to believe I'm standing in a cemetery not all that far from Emily Dickinson's grave, and I'm wearing her clothes.

"Tate," I say between gulps for air, "I think I know what you're thinking."

"I don't think you have *any* idea . . ."

"You're thinking I belong in a psych ward—"

"Not even close, Claire. I'm thinking of *other* things, and the first is how I'm going to get you home in that dress."

"I don't live far . . ."

"And you're going to walk down Pleasant Street in December in a dress that's a hundred years old while the police most likely are scouring the neighborhood?"

"Oh, right. I'll have to take it off."

"Claire, we don't have a lot of time to argue about this. But are you wearing—a shirt under there?"

"Uh-oh." I can feel the cold night air on my skin through the cotton. "Oh, Tate," I gasp. "I left my shirt and my sweater behind at the house. We'll have to go get them—" Even before it's out of my mouth I realize how impossible getting back the evidence of the past hour will be, how much new trouble I can now be in. The night suddenly gets even colder.

"Are you cr—" He stops short. I can hear the panic in his voice, his breathing still not back to normal. "Listen, you have to be very still here in the bushes while I run to my dorm and get my car."

"What—the police—what if they have tracking dogs and they get my scent from my shirt?"

"Claire, *this is Amherst*," he says. "Stay still. You'll be okay. I run fast."

I listen to his footsteps pounding on the ground until I can't hear them anymore. While I wait for the hounds of hell to find me, I pray for the first time since Richy disappeared. I look at the moon, directly over the cemetery, and I pray for something I never imagined I might pray for.

Please, help Tate hurry back.

I can see the blue lights hurrying down Triangle Street and hear the sirens starting, the way they blend and melt into each other. I can feel the ache at the back of my throat from running and the cold. It feels like a knife. I close my eyes. The sirens grow louder.

Hurry, Tate.

I press my eyes closed, hard. The sirens rewind things.

She'll be okay, I kept saying.

If they come fast, she'll be okay.

She'll be okay again this time. If they come.

And then I heard them, how many of them were coming, how they were coming from all directions.

There must have been twenty sirens—I could hear—swirling and lacing around the house. I kept saying hurry.

Hurry.

Even though a part of me knew there was no reason to hurry.

A part of me knew this time was different. That part of me was growing with every second. That part was swelling and taking over the rest. By the time they got there, that part of me was all that was left. I already knew that not even a hundred of them could change the fact that this time was different.

I knew I had come too late.

She was gone.

I see the bright blue lights stabbing through the hemlock branches. If they look here—if they know to look here—they will surely find me.

Hurry.

Then I see headlights, plain headlights, no blue, slow by the cemetery fence. Automatically, I run toward them, not even knowing what kind of car he drives. All I can think of is *Run to the car.* Then the passenger side opens, and I see his face appear from the darkness.

"Fast," he says, as I hop in and slam the door. Instantly blue light rushes over the dashboard and fills up the car. Then the car goes black again as the police car rushes past us.

"That was a close one," Tate says.

I watch the blue lights turn the corner ahead, in the dark. I exhale. My whole body is shaking with the cold.

"I thought"—it's more difficult to get out the words than I expect—"you'd never show up." I take a deep breath, and another. "I thought they'd see me. I couldn't—"

"It's okay. Nobody saw you. Look behind us."

I turn, still shivering. The street behind us is empty.

"See? It's okay."

My teeth chatter uncontrollably. "Do you have an extra shirt or something?"

"I didn't have time to get anything—I thought it was more important to get you out of sight." He reaches for the switch and I hear the heater fan click into high. I watch his hands move to the bottom of his sweatshirt, which he pulls over his shoulders in an efficient movement. "Take this."

"No."

His sweatshirt is in a loose puddle of cloth around his neck.

"I mean—it's freezing," I say. "You can't be—uh—naked in the car." I swallow, looking straight ahead at the road. "If anyone sees—if the police see, they'll stop you. Just for being—odd."

I can hear him take a deep breath. The light turns green and he drives straight ahead, the sweatshirt still pooled around his neck. I'm trying to keep my eyes on the path of the headlights, the road we're on that's leading through the university and out of town.

"I could turn back to my dorm," he says, reinserting his hands, one at a time, through the sleeves. It smells like a camping trip in the car now, like boys and mold.

"No," I say, louder than I expect.

"I'll just park outside and—"

"I'll take care of it. Myself. I have Tess—"

"What? No. Claire, no one else can know—"

"I have to call her," I say. "It's the only way." I'm starting to hear the fear in my words now, the way my voice sounds tinny and distant, like another girl's. "I know I can trust *her*," I say quietly.

Tate stops and looks at me. He must have heard the same girl in the car with him, with that voice. He hands me his cell phone. He's shaking his head while he does it.

"Tess," I say, "I—I need your help."

Tate dims his headlights as we turn onto Cosby Street. I tell him to pull in just before the hedges. I don't know if it's because being in this car is so awkward and silent or because I'm afraid to move in this dress, but I feel I have to conserve my breathing—as if I need to take up as little of the resources of this car as I can. I believe Tess may not ever come out. I see the silhouettes of Tess's parents in the living room and blue TV light. Maybe Tess is popping corn for the nuclear family.

Finally, I hear the crunch of footsteps and she knocks on my window.

I open my door. She glances at me and her eyes get huge. Before I have a chance to speak, she says, "You *have* been working on your writing. So where are you and Ralph Waldo Emerson headed tonight?" And she shoves a pink oxford shirt and fleece at me. It's painful that she's chuckling. "I'll get the details tomorrow. I gotta get back before my parents find you two— Okay, you kids have fun!" I hear her feet crunching on what's left of the snow in her yard as she runs to the back door. "It was just the dog in the yard," she yells.

* * *

The mixture of the cold outside air and the heat of the car has steamed up the glass so that the windshield is nothing but a numb blur of gray mixed with blue streetlight. I close my eyes again.

If I don't open them, this whole night could be untrue. It could be just something I thought once when I was bored. I try to stay very still. But when the automatic breathing clicks in and I happen to inhale normally, reality wafts back with the scent of this stranger's car and this old dress that seems to be coming back to life with my body heat.

It's like I'm in a car with three strangers. One of them is me.

I hear him ask, "What?"

I open my eyes. A patch of the world is coming into focus on the windshield just over the dashboard. The rest of the fog is morphing into drops that make their way down the frosted glass in crooked night-colored lines. "I was just wondering how this happened."

He exhales one brief, decisive breath. That's his reply, I guess. He begins a series of movements, banging on the vent first, and then I feel the direction of the hot air change, aiming upward. He releases the brake next and reaches for the front window with his left hand. I watch his bare hand make a big sloppy mess of the fog, changing it to blurry glass. Now we're underwater, and he's exchanged one problem for another.

Tate drives to a parking lot near the university. "Coast is clear," he says.

"I'm going to have to get out of the car and get into the backseat to change," I say. He's looking straight ahead. Even in this light, I can see the stiffness in his jaw. "So could you just pull the car around to a place where no one will see me change?" I say. "Please."

The car moves closer to some trees near a brick building.

Once I'm in the backseat, I look in the rearview mirror, where I see a slice of his face. I clear my throat. His eyes show up in the mirror. "Uh," I say, "could you—?"

He dramatically squeezes his eyes shut.

It's not as easy getting the dress off, now that I've been cold and then very warm. I slowly work the sleeves off first, and then I pull the dress over my head, trying hard not to see it—to see any damage or to look at the buttons on the dress. The buttons, especially, make this whole thing so much more real. It's those *buttons* that make my whole chest turn to lead. With effort I manage to change into the clothes Tess gave me and roll up the sleeves. And then I stop. I look at the dress on my lap.

I have Emily Dickinson's dress on my lap in Tate's backseat.

I really do.

"Do you think it's okay to fold it?" I'm wondering, but I must say this out loud, too.

"I don't think it's okay to touch it at all," he says. "Ever." I can see in the mirror, his eyes are still smashed shut. The lead area of my body expands.

"It's late," he says in a rusty voice. "Your par—"

"My *father*," I correct him.

"Oh—I—"

"My father has probably already been contacted by the police, who identified my DNA they found on my sweater and T-shirt."

Did Tate just laugh?

"Do you think they use the same crime lab as the cops on *CSI Miami*?" He's shaking his head. "Look, we're not going to figure

68

this out tonight, and being out here could make it worse. Leave the dress with me."

"No way," I say. "It's not your deal."

"Of course it's my deal. You're not walking into your father's house with Emily Dickinson's dress tonight, Claire. That's just not happening."

"It's safer at the dorm?"

He turns toward me. I can see just a portion of his face around the headrest. "Fold the dress—*carefully*—and put it into my backpack and I'll lock it in the trunk. We'll return it in the morning."

I can feel how hard I'm biting my lip.

"We'll figure it out. Somehow. And Claire—" He's looking at me in the back, around the headrest. I can only see half his face. "Why don't you come and sit in the front seat now?"

I am relieved to know my father is already gone when I wake up. I don't know what else to do, so I go to Emily Dickinson's grave. There are two women there in identical black ponchos— *Coincidence? Or are they some kind of hit squad?*—and they are bearing flowers.

"Did you hear about the dress?" one asks me. Of course, since I'm at the grave I'm part of the club. I should know that from past experience. She starts to tell me the story. The plot is *my* evening last night, except in her version it's a fraternity prank and the drunks got away with a vintage piece of Americana.

"It's just a shame they forgot about the security cameras," one of them says.

CAMERAS?

I can feel all the blood pooling in the center of my chest, imagining the movie of last night.

But then, relief. My heart pumps again, surges, in fact, along the top of my head.

The shame is that the cameras had been turned *off* for her birthday celebration the week before. The *they* is the people who run the house.

No cameras.

The women go back and forth about what might be adequate punishment. They are counting up the jail term in five-year increments, depending on whether there was premeditation.

"It's like someone was murdered," one of them says.

I need to see Tate.

I have my hood pulled up and I'm sitting on a bench near the common, where there's something going on for kids and their teddy bears. I'm afraid of what Tate might be doing—having coffee with Perzan or visiting the police—but I try not to think about it. I'm sleepy and my legs hurt from the running and the hiding. I keep hearing Tate's last words to me: *We'll figure it out. Somehow.*

We'll figure it out? We don't even have each other's cell numbers. This figuring out is going badly. Is it even good to be sitting in the middle of a children's party with my hood up, or is it more likely that it makes me a suspect for almost any crime? It's just a matter of minutes before my miserable life gets even worse, I'm thinking.

And then I remember: *My backpack.*

My journal.

My name.

Oh. No. That's worse than a sweater and T-shirt. Way worse.

I left my backpack behind the trash can. The police could have it right now . . . I run, my heart thumping, through the crowd of kids and bears, to the alley.

I see the big square garbage can and have to stop myself. I stand there trying to look bored, and when the coast is clear I practically dive behind the trash.

Ah, it's there. I open it and do a quick inventory: there's my journal. I turn back to the street and walk into something very solid. The impact makes my head go black.

When my eyes adjust, I see it's Tate.

Neither of us says anything until we are out of Amherst, on Route 9, in his car heading over the Connecticut River. But then both of us speak at the exact same time.

Me: "What were *you* doing at Emily Dickinson's house?"

Tate: "What were you doing *at Emily Dickinson's house?*"

"I was there because you were there," Tate says, with more than just a little anger brewing in his voice.

"I go because—"

"What do you mean 'go'?"

I explain I've been there a lot, that the window lifts easily and that I've never had any trouble before. "I started going after I read . . . Wait a minute, what do you mean *you* were there because I was there? How did you know where I was?"

"I followed you," he says.

"Okay, that's more than a little creepy," I say.

He continues as if I hadn't said anything. "I was worried when

I saw you throw your backpack away. And then I lost you when you got to the house. I walked around the house for a long time, and just when I was going to give up, I saw you through the window. The look on your face . . . I was sure you . . ."

He stops. He pulls into a parking space across from Thornes Marketplace in Northampton.

I know what he was about to say: *I was sure you were going to self-destruct.*

"You were sure I was going to hurt myself. You read my writing and you know my story and you reached a conclusion. A logical conclusion."

I am looking at a street musician, focusing very hard on the rainbows on his head scarf. The man's dog seems to be weary with this day, as I am. I open my window and hang my whole arm out. The slow mandolin music is sad, an appropriate score considering what Tate thinks of me.

And then suddenly, Tate bursts out laughing. He is laughing so hard the car shakes. Even the musician's dog looks over.

"It's perverse—" he says, stopping so he can continue his episode of explosive laughter. The pretend teacher who followed a student last night is starting a sentence like that?

"It's perverse that I'm so glad you went there to steal Emily Dickinson's dress, that you weren't there to hurt yourself." His laughter spasms are slowing. He sighs at the end.

I let him finish. I feel my fists clenching. "I wasn't there to hurt myself or to steal the dress. *You* forced me to run."

"But you were wearing the dress."

"I go there all the time. It was tempting. I wasn't going to keep—"

"You go there all the time to wear the dress?"

"No, I go there . . . well . . . I started to go there for the story. I was going to write about what happened to Emily Dickinson, to imagine why no one ever saw her—why there was just the one photograph. I wanted to use the layout of the house in the story . . . And then I kept going because—" I stop, think about how to say it so it doesn't sound as crazy as it will. "You're not going to understand this, but I'm going to say it because it's true. I go there because . . . I feel close to my mom. *Like she's there, too.*"

I fight the urge to blink my eyes shut, and I look at him, right into his eyes.

To my surprise, he nods. "No, no, I get that. I do."

"You do?"

"But how do you *not* set off the alarm?"

"I don't know," I say. "I come in through the window that they leave open. How did *you* set the alarm off?"

"When I saw you through the window, I could just barely make you out. But I panicked. I couldn't find how you'd gotten in. I ran to the back door and I—uh—*tried* it."

"You *tried* it?"

"Okay, I tried it *hard.*"

"So I ran out of the house in the dress because you thought I had snapped, and now we both have stolen the dress of one of the world's most beloved poets?"

"Yep, that sounds about right."

He lays his forehead on the steering wheel. "I didn't know how I would get to you this morning. I couldn't go to your house without having to explain who I am to your father. I mean, what do I say? *Hello, I'm the student teacher in your daughter's English class, and she and I accidentally ran off with Emily Dickinson's dress?* I was walking in circles."

I hear him groan. His hands are on his head, which is still on the steering wheel. "Oy," he mutters. "This is *very* bad."

Until I hear the fiddler, I don't think much about the crowd on the street. The fiddler has come to join the mandolin player. They are kicking up a storm. A group has started to gather, complete with a festive party atmosphere. And Mr. Perzan. He's tapping his foot. Surprisingly, he's a music lover.

Fancy meeting you here.

I slowly shrink into my seat.

"Uh, Tate?"

He lifts his head off the steering wheel just enough so I can see part of his face. "What?"

"Mr. Perzan at three o'clock." I gesture with my head.

Tate shoots up.

The fiddler really takes off. The engine starts. I hear the motor of my window whir. I monitor what's going on by watching Tate's poker face. From this angle I can see he needs a shave.

"All clear," he says once we are out of town and on 91. The miles around us are houseless and therefore fearless, just squares and rectangles in muted colors, a faded quilt. He rolls down the windows and we both take deep breaths of the cold air.

I lean against the car door, trying to be minimal in the picture, almost like an afterthought. Tate's jaw is set tight. I can see out of the corner of my eye how firmly he clenches the steering wheel, and the car *is* going faster with each passing minute.

"Do you—have any brothers or sisters?" I ask.

"*What?*"

Up ahead, it seems to be snowing on the mountains of Vermont. The sky is dull, and the lumpy clouds look like overfilled gray sacks. *Come on, Tate. Say something back, Tate. Please make small talk.*

The speedometer says 80. It probably would be better not to be stopped by the police . . .

"I don't . . . have any," I say in a small voice. "I wish . . . I did."

There is this long moment of silence, and then I hear him start up. "Maggie was first." He says this slowly, like this fact requires accuracy. "I came one year later, and then Ben, the year after me. He's a sophomore at Penn."

"Middle child," I say. "The puzzle pieces fall into place . . ."

This makes him smile, and the car slows down a bit. "Not really," he says. He speaks in a new voice, one I haven't heard before. "We were so close in age, and my parents divorced when we were really young. We pretty much only had one another."

"Um. Sorry about that," I say. "But it's good you had . . . *company.*"

"It's always good to have company," he says, nodding. Something about him looks sad. I allow myself to study that look before I turn to face the road. I should really try to keep my eyes ahead.

It gets quiet again, with just the sound of the engine. "Claire," he starts. "I know this is weird. I don't want it to be weird."

"I'm pretty sure I have no control over the abundance of weird in my life," I say. "I've actually given that a good deal of thought."

"Why did you run out of that coffee place?" Out of the corner of my eye, I see he turns to me. He seems genuinely puzzled. "That *was* weird. It was scary. You looked so . . ."

"*You* followed me," I say. *Because that's what happened.* That's what's true. I turn to him to punctuate this with a blank face.

"What was I *supposed* to do?" His new voice is ragged.

"I'm not a project," I say. "I'm not some kind of problem for you and Perzan to sort through. You and Perzan know a lot more than I'd intended . . . now that you told him . . ."

His whole face twists, his eyebrows pulling together tightly. His hand roughly flicks on the turn signal and we head for an exit. His chest moves quickly up and down. He's very angry about what I said.

The car lurches to a stop, jerking me forward. Tate, however, has a firm grip on the steering wheel. Like the car, he's made of steel. He snaps off the ignition. He turns to face me.

"I didn't tell Perzan anything," he says. "You assumed I did. You do that kind of thing a lot. You know? You fly off the handle, Claire. You jump to conclusions."

I feel myself tensing up.

"And another thing. You firmly believe you are the center of everything. You are *convinced* of that. You know what? You aren't the only person in the world, Claire. Even though you have had a terrible life—maybe your life is even a horror story still—but you aren't the only one who's ever lost someone—I did—I—do—I have something at stake here, too. I could get kicked out of Amherst in my junior year because of this. Does any of this register with you? Does anybody else *ever* matter to you?"

The air is sucked from my chest. I feel my mouth open, but air does not enter.

"You told me your story for a reason, Claire. At first, I didn't even believe it. Then you told me more. You wanted somebody to know. And you ran out of that place because *you knew I would follow you—*"

I need to breathe, need air. I can reach for the door handle, pull, feel my shoulder push on the door—

"NO." His hand grips my left wrist. "YOU ARE NOT DOING THIS AGAIN," he yells. He reaches over and now he's gripping my arm with both hands as I'm pulling away, trying to breathe. I quickly pull my hand from the door.

Oh. Oh. My hand is a hard ball. It's fist-shaped and flying through the air. It's flying toward Tate's face.

Chapter 8

THERE IS BLOOD.

I seem to have been the cause.

Tate has his hands over his face. He seems to be moaning. I do see blood between his fingers. I have air in my lungs now, in fact, too much. I seem to need to get rid of it.

My hand throbs.

His hands move down his face. He looks at me.

He moves his hands so his fingers surround his nose but his mouth can move. "Claire—hyberbetilatig."

Hyberbetilatig?

He's saying something is happening to him. Something bad.

*Hyper*ventilating.

He's hyperventilating?

"But I don't know CPR!" I gasp.

He takes one bloody hand off his face and holds it up. He touches my shoulder. Slow. Steady. He covers his nose with the other hand, his eyes looking straight into mine. Despite all this, there's a straight line from his meaningful green eyes to mine.

Yes, I see them.

I see blood, too.

His voice sounds as if it comes from the inside of a cave. "Claire." It's a calm cave voice. "You're hyberbetilatig. It's all right. Dough Buddy's dead."

Dough Buddy's dead?

Who's Dough Buddy?

Oh. *Nobody's* dead.

Hhhh—I feel the first kick to my gut, a rumbling. I lean forward into it. It erupts from way inside my middle and shoots out in coughs. I nearly choke. I am laughing hard, with everything I have, bent over laughing, shaking and laughing and rocking onto my knees. Laughing so hard I'm crying.

I feel something sticky on my head.

I look up. It's Tate's hand, his bloody fingers sticking to my hair.

His eyes are shocked. "Laughig? You're laughig?" He's trying to get my hair untangled from his hand.

It·makes me roar harder.

He's laughing now, untangling his fingers and pulling out my hair, laughing almost as hard as I am, and bleeding, too; a stream leads down his neck and pools at the collar of his shirt.

He's leaning back in his seat, holding his chin up. His face is smeared with blood, and so are his T-shirt and jacket. The shoulder of my hoodie has bloody handprints.

"I'b neber really seed you laugh," he says between gulps of laughing.

I look around, the laughter spasms slowing. Cows across the highway are lined up at a fence watching us. "Where are we?"

"Verbot," he says. "We crossed the border a couple of biles back."

"*Vermont?* Oh my God," I say. I take off my hoodie and offer it to him for his face. "You'd better let me drive. You're a bloody mess and we've just crossed the state line with Emily Dickinson's dress." I reach for the door handle. "I guess we have to go back to Amherst and find you a doctor," I say.

"I dough you're dot big on obeyig laws, but could you dot speed or anything? We dowt wat to get stopped with that dress id the car."

Once I figure out what he's saying, I shake my head and start the engine. "Yeah," I say, remembering. "The *dress.*"

The snow sky from Vermont seems to be traveling with us, its gray veil turning the day into something cast in iron. The hand I punched Tate with aches. I look at Tate, whose nose is skyward, whose face is almost completely covered up by my hoodie. His whole face is probably throbbing, too. And it's because of me. He most likely has a terrible headache.

I could ask him about how he's feeling, show him I'm not the center of my own universe, offer to take the next exit, and head off through nowhere looking for Advil. I try to get myself to do that. But instead I find myself concentrating on the dull highway, made more dull by the bad light. I hear him moving and look over. He's testing different head positions.

"I think it's stopped," he says, sounding less interior.

"I'm—I guess I'm sorry," I say, glancing over at him. He is a very bloody guy.

"No you're not," he says, looking out the passenger window.

"I know," I say. "But I thought it would make you feel better if I said it." I smile. "See? I'm thinking about how you might be feeling—I'm not completely self-absorbed."

He looks over at me. "Do you fight a lot?" he asks. "Knife fights and stuff?"

I snort. We pass fields of apocalyptic cornstalks. "When," I ask, "back there, what you said about how at first you didn't believe me—when did you decide that I wasn't lying?"

He laughs. It's a short burst of laughter, though, and ends up in a gurgle. It seems to hurt. "You're convinced that I have made that decision once and for all?"

I shrug. "Good point. You haven't seen enough of my bizarre life for the prequel to make sense. I get it."

"Ha." He flinches.

"I'm telling you. I swear it's all true." I raise my hand, and I notice it's red and starting to swell. "I was born under this really bad star, on a day when the chickens were walking backwards and my mother was . . ." I don't finish this sentence. Even though I was going to make a joke about my mother, I have to leave the attempt incomplete. Maybe forever.

"I've read your writing. *Something* happened."

"You know, it's not fair—that you get to read it. It's like being in a room with a one-way mirror. You can see me, but I can only see myself."

"That's the way things are with writers and their readers," he says.

I sigh. "Do you want some Advil?" I ask. "I think there's a drug-store in Deerfield. I was going to stop and get some—for my hand."

Minutes later he's tucked into his seat, holding a cold bottle of water against his forehead.

"We'll be there in twenty minutes," I say, starting the car.

"So why did they think you had something to do with it?" he asks. "When your friend ran away—"

"Ran away . . ." I repeat those words. "I like that version. Did I call it that?"

It was real winter, Tate, I could say. I've gone over the story so many times in exactly this way, trying to figure it out. *It was real winter, the last day I saw him. The sky was the right gray.* Ducks were swimming in a small thaw in the ice stream behind the mall. The runoff water was a toxic shade of orange, as usual. The ducks were surrounded by ice that looked like broken glass. It was a dangerous-looking picture, the drab birds and the glass shards. Richy had just emptied a whole box of Tic-Tacs into the water. The ducks dived among the broken ice and into the water, quack-ing and arguing before pointing their behinds skyward.

"You've driven them to cannibalism," I said.

"I have that effect on wildlife," Richy said.

But, Tate, we made plans for that night. We stood there and made plans. That's what seventeen-year-old kids do. Even ones who aren't quite average make plans for the night. *No one was running away that night.*

"Or—disappeared," he says. He shakes his head and pinches his eyes shut. Maybe it's from the pain. "Forget it," he says, "I didn't mean to—"

"I was the last person to see Richy," I say. "And they knew that. People saw me with him. Behind the mall. But I lied."

"You lied?"

"I lied. I told them I didn't see him."

"Why? If you didn't have anything to do with it, why lie?"

"Because of my mother. She—"

How do I say this so you understand how these two things connect? And how to say it so you don't think she was horrible? *She was not horrible. She was never horrible.*

"My life with my mother was not ever a horror story," I begin. "It was tragic, but not horrible. Not ever." I feel my throat get clogged up, and I cough to clear it out. "In so many ways it was wonderful. But"—I swallow—"she tried to kill herself. Three times. The third time, she was successful."

"Successful," he says. It's definitely not a question.

Good. You're following along.

"Each time I was alone with her." I look at him. I check to see it's still clear what I mean. "The first two times, I saved her. *You know?* The third time . . ."

"I get it," he says. He reaches a hand out in my direction.

Even though he seems to want me to stop before he hears this part, I take a good, long, deep breath. "That time I failed," I say.

"Failed?"

"Everybody in town knew the whole story. They thought I was—well, *scarred* would be a nice way to put it. And there were others who thought—worse of me. That I cause things."

He gives up and his hand drops down. He's really got it now.

"Let's just say it was hard," I say, "to get playdates."

Chapter 9

THE TRICKY PART is that our house in Amherst has a short driveway that curves around hedges. If you are in the house, you see everyone who enters the driveway even before they see the house. I am driving myself home to change my clothes so I can drop Tate off at his infirmary, and as I pull into the driveway there are two cars there. One is not so much a surprise. It's my dad's car. The other is marked STATE PATROL.

"NO."

"Oh." I hear him let one of those whistle breaths escape.

"I'm taking the blame," I say, stopping the car before I even reach the front of the house. "It was all my fault." I quickly reach for the car door and slam it behind me. The stupid thing I do is open the back to get the pack with the dress. This slows me up, so I can't get to the front door of the house first. Tate, even though he's shaky, is right by my side, slipping in next to me.

"Claire, what's going on? Where have you been? Was there a car accident?" My father is rushing toward me. Tate is practically sewn to my arm. I notice my dad can't keep his eyes off my shirt, which was light green once, and now is green hand-printed with blood. Actually, I notice that both Tate and I are wearing a good deal of blood.

I also notice there are two large men in the room. They have hats and big black boots. They must be the matching pair that comes with the car with the lights mounted on top.

"No—no car accident. Everything is fine," I say without a trace of irony. I feel Tate's sharp fingers digging into my arm.

"What *happened* to you?" He can't stop looking at my hair now. *What is going on with my hair?*

"Who is this?" he asks, turning now to Tate, who looks a lot like a zombie. His face is swollen and lumpy and red and covered with streaks of dried blood.

The two matching men step over. They are quietly inspecting us—Tate more than me. From a law-enforcement perspective, this makes some sense.

"A boyfriend," I say. Instantly, I amend that. "*My* boyfriend." I feel Tate let go of my arm. "We had a fight. It got a little out of control." I keep my eyes on the rug. There are a lot of feet in this small room.

"*Boyfriend?*" my father asks.

"She's got *some* temper," Tate says.

I notice Tate's hand appearing just over my shoulder. I watch as he pats my shoulder in a really awkward, third-grade way. It's a surreal gesture, considering that in a matter of seconds the hand-cuffs will appear. I can hear them clicking as they lock—first on my wrists then his. My heart's beating fast, but I'm trying not to show it. I pay attention to every detail: I look over at my dad to see if the first shots will come from that direction. But I notice now that he seems too worn out for a showdown. In fact, he looks as if a tornado just tore through his body, from the inside out. I see that his glasses are slightly off kilter, and his hair seems to have been uprooted and then set down funny. It's got to be more than the bogus-boyfriend news or even the blood. Though there is a lot of blood.

He knows about the dress. We're going to jail. Let's get this over with. I don't think my heart can take any more.

But something is stalled out, as if the projectionist has forgotten the second reel and we have to kill time in the dark. I reach behind my shoulder to the strap of the backpack. I scoop it around to the front of me, into my arms, like a shield. At the same time I brace myself, I search the perimeter the way you naturally do during panic—you look for holes in the hedges and gaps in the fence. Places to run toward. I pull the backpack closer to my chest as I'm scanning the room for one of those escape holes—maybe I can pull Tate through, too: *all I need is one*—when I notice, through the window, the police car.

It says Rhode Island State Police.

Why would Rhode Island police be interested in Emil—?

I squeeze the backpack to my chest, harder.

Hhhhhh.

"Ri-chy," I say. The name cracks in half as it comes out. You can almost see the two pieces.

Why didn't I think of this right away?

"You found—?" This part I say in a much smaller voice. If I don't ever completely ask this question—if I only partially ask—then I won't ever completely have the answer. It's been like that for almost a year, the cocktail of not-knowing. That mixture of fear and hope. Right now I believe it's better than having the answer. Right now I am certain of that.

Because I do know now. I know from the look on my father's face. The wrinkles in his face are more like ruts, like gouges.

I do know now, and it is worse.

I feel my hand throbbing, pulsing, like a heart that hurts. I let go of the backpack. Just the strap catches on my arm, and it gently falls to the ground and settles down near my toes.

I'm surrounded by these men—my father, Tate, the two officers—with Emily Dickinson's dress at my feet, when I say the wrong thing, as usual. I say, "Oh. Not *Richy*—" No one would be sorry if they found Richy. There would be a parade. *"His body."*

The officers, both of them, move their big black boots a tiny step forward—you could miss it if you weren't paying attention—and then at the same time they both lean closer, watching me. They are just waiting for what I might say next.

"Where?" I ask.

That they don't require me to ride in the police car elates my father. He points out the positive nature of our liberty to drive to Providence in the comfort of his Subaru.

After all, that's what America is about.

As an American, was I required to say to the police, *Thank you for letting me ride in my Subaru instead of in the cage of your backseat?* It's been a while since I've been called to a police station for "an interview"—though not nearly the time span of my whole life, as I'd hoped—and I've forgotten the etiquette.

"When we get there, don't say anything odd," my dad reminds me.

Odd?

"Is it *what* I say or *how* I say it that makes things odd?" I ask for clarification of the rules.

He then points out that he's glad the seat warmers are fully functional, because it *is* chilly. I'm remembering that he's fairly random when he's hysterical. And his hair is still looking crooked. I can't figure that part out, but he has got some color in his cheeks.

I, on the other hand, appear quite pale. I note this as I look in the side mirror. There's me in this mirror, looking pale—at this point I note that I have blood in my hair—Tate's blood from when he put his hand on my head when he thought I was crying.

Too bad I didn't see the clotted blood in my hair—I could have washed it, or even cut it. I would have a very large chunk of hair missing if I'd cut it, and that would call my character into question: What sort of girl has a chunk of hair missing?

Why does blood dry so fast, and why am I repeating other parts of my life besides chemistry class—like revisiting Providence police stations?

Some other questions will require further thought:

1. When I go to the police station and the whole thing starts up again, will the fact that I have congealed blood in my hair affect the way my answers are viewed?
2. Will it be like the first time I went to the police station, the time I lied?
3. Will I lie?
4. For example, if asked about the last time I saw Richy, what will I say?

a. Behind the mall, there was ice in the water and there were ducks.
b. He was meeting a dentist later.
c. He had first met the dentist over the Internet.
d. He was nervous about it and I was coming along, but I was late. I'll say it this time. I'll tell them.
e. All of the above.

"Dad, can we stop at the McDonald's over there? I need a soda. I need something to drink." He doesn't seem to hear me. I try more persuasive material. "And I need to use the bathroom."

I'll tell them about how I was late.

How I do these things.

How I fail, and how people disappear quickly—even more quickly than blood coagulates.

"Didn't you say something odd last time? Didn't you say that for Richy sad is normal?" my dad asks. "I remember them saying that about you. That you think sad can be normal." He has his verb tenses mixed up.

It *was* normal. *Sad was normal for Richy.* It's easy to mix up verb tenses with the dead.

What makes blood so sticky?

What does it mean that when Tate thought I was crying because Dough Buddy was dead that he put his hand on my head? I could feel how softly he did that—even though I'd just punched him hard enough to probably break his nose. I could feel how gentle he was. If I close my eyes, I still can.

But when I do that, I see Richy's leather jacket floating on the water. Washing up near the docks.

"And tell me again who that guy was—why did you need to lie to the police about him being your boyfriend? It's worse than saying odd things. You know that, right? That lying to the police is worse than saying odd things?"

"Dad, you need to stop the car." I feel the saliva start to fill up my mouth. I can barely get this out: "I'm going to throw up—now."

I can feel my heart beating as I press my hands on the table and my chest against my hands. I can feel the zipper of my jacket and my heart beating hard. The officer, across the table from me, seems to have allergies. He has trouble opening his eyes.

"On that night . . ." the officer says, aiming his face over the top of me, like looking at my face is unimportant.

On that night.

"At first you said you weren't with him on that night—"

"I was with him. Earlier." *That afternoon he was wearing his leather jacket. It was so cold. And he wore those shoes he was afraid would get scuffed up, and those bright green socks with orange diamonds.*

The officer's eyes start to aim at mine. They are small, shiny black beans. "At first you told us you didn't see him after school. You said—"

"I was wrong," I say too quickly to give it any thought, and stop just as fast when I hear the word *wrong* echo across the vastness of the enormous table.

"Wrong?"

I let out a breath. "I lied. I was wrong when I lied."

"So you are saying you lied to the police last February, when Richard DiMarco was reported missing?"

"I'm saying it *again*," I say. "I told them then. I told them I don't know why I lied. Maybe because I felt guilty—"

"Guilty?" He's leaning back. I notice how floppy the skin of his face is, like a balloon that has lost most of its air, the two black beans tucked into the creases.

"Not that kind of guilty. I felt—responsible . . ."

Now his shiny eyes are steady, locked on my face. There must be some training for how to look someone in the eye without blinking.

"I mean—I was late. I was supposed to meet him, and I was late. He had left already. I was supposed to go, too. He played the phone message from the dentist. I heard it. I said I want to come, too, because it didn't seem right. I was supposed to be there . . ."

There is silence in the room for a long time. The shiny beans seem to be doing some kind of calculation. "Dentist?" he asks.

"I said all of this before," I say. I can hear my voice rise. "You didn't know this already? It's not in some kind of file? I told the police back then—when he was just missing and not—" My mouth is very dry, I notice. I can hear myself trying to swallow. "He met the dentist over the Internet," I tell him, even though it's all been said before. "That's exactly what he told me. It's all he told me. And I heard the phone message, about them meeting."

"Uh-huh. And did he ever say that he was tired of everything?"

And then I hear a laugh—it's my laugh—because who doesn't say that at some time? But he was making plans. He was playing guitar all of a sudden. He was singing. *He was a terrible singer,* I want to say. *But it didn't stop him.*

He was becoming someone new, you see? He wanted to become someone new.

The officer leans back. He seems to have officially reached a conclusion. He's aiming his beans over my head again.

"So he *did* sometimes say that he was tired of things?"

"Yeah—but did anyone look for the dentist? There had to be some kind of phone records that could link to the dentist," I say. "Did you check the phone records?"

"We checked all that out last February," he says. "And did he say it a lot?"

"Did he say what?"

"That he was tired of things."

I allow one of my hands to fold over the other.

"What's a lot?" I say, joining him in his lack of imagination. I don't even bother to explore the wrinkles in his skin to look for eyes. Instead, I stare at the poster on the wall behind him. It's been partially ripped down. All that's left is 8 SIGNS OF. The rest of the title is missing. I can only imagine what it might have said.

"More than once?" he asks again. His voice is so matter-of-fact.

"Yeah," I say, looking at the remnants of the poster. I'm starting to decide whether a suspect or an officer tore it. "He said it all the time."

Chapter 10

WEEKS HAVE MOVED BY in an underwater way, without sound. My father starts to ask a question about the day we heard about Richy, but the scene turns wordless and ends with him carefully patting the top of my head.

I'm walking past the Unitarian church that's not far from the cemetery where you can find Emily Dickinson's grave when I realize that in this part of my life I've become a scarecrow. It's been like this since that day the police came to the house—I have holes in me, and wind blows through. Oh, I seem to be person-shaped all right, but I'm going nowhere.

The only thing I can think of is:

This is the way people leave.

They leave without saying much.

The wind blows them off to sea.

Just today, Saturday, the streets have started to fill up with bright hats: the students are staggering back into the picture after the holidays, becoming obstacles again, making it hard for scarecrows to maneuver. I keep my straw head down. Because of this, I bump into Tess's Gus, the glassblower. I go flying backwards. I see tiny stars as this happens and hear the wind inside my head, and his laughing.

"Why are you walking on the street with your head down?" he asks. "Are you looking for money on the ground?"

He puts his big hands on my arms and sets me up straight. I'd forgotten how large he is, how he's like a giant. "I'm going to get you some hot chocolate," he says, taking my arm. He leads me across the street to the Amazing Bean. He props me up at a table and brings me a white mug topped with an abundance of froth. He sits across from me. There's something European in the way he gives me something warm and nourishing and sits back to watch, grinning.

In Europe do they smile all winter? I wonder.

"Tess says she hasn't seen you. She'll be needing a friend, I think."

I look at him and his charcoal eyebrows, the way his face smiles all the time. It makes me feel less like a scarecrow.

"I know she's been busy," I say. "*You* keep her busy." I smile. "Besides, I've had this college stuff. Long car trips with my dad." I shrug. "I'll call her."

We are sitting at the back of the shop, in the shadows of an already dim day. Outside, I see these reappearing students on the street, filling the window with their bright parkas and mittens like colorful paws.

They bubble into the coffee shop, making more noise than they need to, so happy to see each other after centuries apart.

"I was just wondering," he says, looking at my hot chocolate. At the front counter, I notice the Amherst College rowing team is gathering, their purple jackets all kinetic and hard to keep straight. It's mostly because they all have honey-colored heads, or seem to.

"If you could, you know, keep track of Tess when I go back to Putney?"

I am looking in Gus's direction but, at the same time, glancing over, sorting through the tangle of rowers. All of them have red cheeks. All of them seem to have already had enough coffee, though they are here for more. Many large paper cups are bobbing around them. When I focus my eyes on Gus, he's staring at me.

"You haven't talked to her lately. She seems really down," he says.

"I'm sorry," I say. "I'll be a better friend. I will. I know you're leaving soon." He reaches across the table and squeezes my arm.

"There's no one in the world like Tess," he says.

"I've been thinking about that a lot," I say.

He laughs. It's a deep laugh, more like rocks tumbling. "I know what you mean," he says, sitting way back in his chair. "I'd like to do something for her before I go," he says. "I'm trying to think of what she'd like. What do you think?"

"Uh—make her something—a cake," I say. I look at my mug. "Bake her a chocolate cake." I force myself to smile. "She'll love that."

He has this way of doing things, like kissing the top of my head while he presses my ears—a head hug—to say thanks. He's the perfect giant from a storybook—a good giant for Tess. That's almost enough to unfreeze me today.

But when he leaves me alone, I'm reminded of the drafts that blow through my scarecrow clothes. I take out my phone and think about dialing Tess, but I can't seem to.

I don't know how to explain one thing without explaining many.

"So where is it?"

I've been having so few conversations lately that it takes me a while to figure out I'm supposed to be a part of this one. By that time, his white paper cup is walking next to me on the street, then his purple jacket is.

"Your nose," I say, turning to him. The wind is taking my breath away, or something is. "I was wondering what happened to it after—" I look at it. But I don't remember much about the way he looked *before* I broke his nose.

All I remember is after. How different the whole world looked.

"It healed. Quickly. See?" He turns his head slowly so I can appreciate his nose from many angles. It has a kind of perfect slope now.

"It looks okay," I say, catching my breath. I feel very warm all of a sudden.

He goes on. "It was a crazy day—a crazy two days—and I left for the holidays, and training with the team, and I didn't have your number or any way to find out what happened—"

"I know. I wanted to tell you about it." I stop walking. "He drowned." I look at the sidewalk, crusted over in snow that had melted and refrozen. "The funny thing is—" As soon as I start to laugh, I'm sorry about the way this whole sentence is going. "They think it was either an accident *or* he might have killed himself." I stop and look at Tate. "What kind of police work is that?"

And how, exactly, is that funny? It's not. Not even a little bit.

Tate's frozen, like everything else. "Oh," I say. I close my eyes and the wind hits my eyelids. "That's not what you meant. You weren't asking—you meant *find out about the dress*—" I nod and change my voice. I lift it. I feel my heart beating hard. "It's in my closet. It's got a few marks on it. I'm trying to figure out how to clean it, or if—"

He's shaking his head. "Is that what *you* think?"

"I'm afraid I'll make things worse if I try," I say, still trying to lift my voice. "It's old cotton—"

"No, not about the dress. About Richy. That he killed himself—is that what *you* think?"

"Ahh. That's complicated," I say, shivering now and feeling a bit nauseated.

"Can we go inside and sit? Do you want to go back to the Amazing Bean?" he asks.

"Back? You were there?"

"I saw you, with your —with that guy. Actually, I've been looking for you today, but I didn't want to interrupt you—I thought you saw me. I waved. But you looked pretty occupied." I'm remembering Gus leaning over to kiss my head and hug my ears with his big hands.

Looking—for me? "I saw your team, but not you." I take a gulp of cold air. "Okay. Let's go."

The Amazing Bean is calmer, dimmer now.

"So you said it's complicated—about Richy. You don't think he killed himself, or do you?"

Tate says these words slowly and so carefully that it's not as hard as it might be to even try to answer the question. "It's a long story," I manage to say. My mouth is dry. I have tea to drink, but it's too hot.

"It's okay," he says. "I have a lot of time."

I take a deep breath. "It was my first day of high school," I begin. My lips drag over my teeth. "I had survived a year of crashing into small pieces, after what happened to my mother. And I woke up re-formed, but you could still see the pieces. I pictured myself like that, like rock candy." I stop. These are the words I have thought of to describe myself, and only now am I saying them for the first time. I was in pieces, but held together somehow. *Like rock candy.* "I thought if I dressed a certain way I could cover up the cracks. It was a new school and I could become anyone I wanted. *No one would know about the cracks.*" I laugh. "The person I chose wore black all the time. She smiled in the wrong places."

"Like now?" he says, only slightly smiling, more like watching with narrow eyes.

"Yes." I blink. I don't look back at his face. I look at the table-top, at two identical mugs of tea. "Anyway, I was walking down this hallway when I heard banging on metal. Then, a locker door opened up and there he was."

He wore yellow high-top sneakers and his hair lay on his forehead like the wing of a blackbird.

"You don't think I look skinny enough to fit in here, do you?" I can hear him in my head. His voice.

"What I was really wondering was how he got in there, though I didn't ask. He squeezed himself out one shoulder at a time and said, *'We are going to be old friends.'* Or was it *odd* friends? He had an accent or a problem pronouncing things. It didn't confuse me as much as it should have. We could be odd friends just as easily as old friends." It didn't matter about the way things came out when he spoke. I always knew what he meant.

"His hair reminded me of a blackbird's wing. Every time he moved his head, the bird's wing fell over his eye. Something about his hair was tragic. I remember using that word in my head."

The table where Gus and I sat is now empty. "It was Tess's glass-blower," I say for no good reason. "Here. Before."

The little crease between his eyes tightens. I touch the edge of the table.

"Gus, her glassblower, said he's leaving for school and that Tess is sad."

"*Tess*—" He seems to be remembering her from a long time ago, looking off in the distance. "What did you tell *her* about the dress?"

"Nothing." I look at my fingers. "Nothing." My fingers are white. They are squeezing the edge of the table. I carefully lay my hands on my lap. "She's been busy. With the holidays and college applications . . . and the glassblower," I say. "And I've been grateful."

"Aren't you afraid she'll tell someone about the dress?"

"I'm more afraid I'll lose her," I say. I find myself laughing. "Much more afraid of that."

"Lose her?"

"She doesn't know any of this stuff—all of these . . . *things*. About Richy. And only some of them about me and my mother. Not to mention the details about the dress."

"You haven't told her *anything*?"

"No."

"Claire, *why*?"

"I've never had a Tess before," I say. "Is it wrong to want one? To want to keep the one I've got?"

He looks up. "You told *me*," he says.

"He—" I look at the tabletop. I see cups, strings for tea bags, and my white fingertips are back. I am holding on tightly. ". . . Richy didn't put *himself* into that locker—it was the kind of thing that happened to him. A lot. He was always either hurting himself or getting hurt."

I let go of the table and pull my hands close to my chest. I wrap my arms around myself. "So, what you asked before . . . No, I don't think Richy killed himself, Tate. I don't think it was an accident, either—they did say something about finding a rope. I told them about the dentist. I told them he said he met a dentist over the Internet. He had that odd way of talking and sometimes things could get mixed up, and all I know is what I heard—what I remember. I do remember. But does that even matter what he said? Does any of it matter now?"

I notice the light inside the Amazing Bean has gradually changed. Now it seems like we're in a dark box with a window on the front. Out that window, snow is falling. "What can I do about him or the way he talked or what he said—or about the dress? What can I do about anything?"

Chapter 11

"I DON'T LIKE DRIVING in the snow." The windshield wipers are very noisy, and the world is white.

"Why? It's nice," says Tate.

"I don't like snow in general. In principle." We drive south along the river, which is black in the middle of all the white. The tree branches hold the snow, so everything is white outlined with black, and even the road is a dark strap that braces the hillside up ahead. "It's not so much *falling* snow, but *fallen* snow I dislike," I say. "It's another burden in a season of burdens . . . short days . . . long nights . . . wet boots . . . wet . . . dogs . . ." I trap a drop of condensed moisture on the glass of the passenger window with my finger. "Where are we going? I should probably have asked."

"On vacation. To Holyoke," Tate says. "We're going to tutor fifth graders. I do that on Saturdays. I thought you might—you know—help me."

"What does that have to do with the dress?"

He shrugs. "I think the dress can wait a bit."

"Oh, I get it—because I'm selfish?" I laugh, just a little. "And you want to rehabilitate me? Ha. You want me to see that not all people are the daughters of college professors, and darn it, lots of inner-city kids have lost a parent and a friend or two?"

"Okay, those reasons would work, too." He smiles, but that crumples up quickly. "Or maybe you're good company on car rides."

I feel my cheeks get hot.

And when I look at him his face is serious, so serious I'd call it a grim face. "I'm sorry for leaving you alone with the dress—that day. I shouldn't have—" He looks at the black road. "It wasn't right."

"What? Don't be silly. I had to go to the police station," I say. "*Again.*"

"But I could have changed my plans to leave for Christmas. I could have—"

"Your nose was broken. I, in fact, broke it. Didn't you need to see a doctor? I mean, it looks okay now." I look at him but turn away before he might notice. "And my father was wondering who the zombie was—he still is, really—and you were *almost my teacher.* It's not as if we're going to have each other's phone numbers or anything, and—" I stop and listen to that last part. I take a breath. "And I was the one wearing the dress. You said it yourself."

"Stop," he says. "The truth is that I was—am—as responsible as you."

I look at the snow that lands in clumps on the windshield, clumps that only for a split second look like gunshots through the glass. Then they surrender, melting. "And so my consolation prize is getting to tutor fifth graders?"

He raises his eyebrows. "It's all I have to offer."

"It's sooo generous," I say. I find myself trying hard not to smile.

"And how about some pizza afterwards?"

"O-kay."

But then I hear him say: "After the vacation is over, though—you're going to talk to Tess, right? You need to tell her the story, so she understands why you—why the two of us—have that dress. That we weren't out to steal it?"

I feel the coldness of winter radiating through the window just when he says her name. Now I get it, what this is about: He's handling me. He's keeping track of things that need to be done. I'll bet he has a checklist somewhere.

I'm a problem, being managed. A project that needs straightening out, again.

"She'd never—"

"Just in case," he says. "She should know why we were—*together*. How it happened. That nobody was planning it."

I look at the cold window near my face and stare at the bottom, where the glass meets the door. "She won't think anything about us—and the dress. I mean, why would she?"

"Just get it straight with her. Explain that it was a bunch of co-incidences."

I nod slowly. "Of course."

"And I'm sorry about leaving you that day, *really*—"

I look over at him and see he's looking at me. I try to understand that look.

"Without taking it off your hands first," he adds. "Maybe you should give it to me now, and then you'll be in the clear."

"W-what do you mean in the clear? We both—" I stop. I feel

my hands tightening up. Oh, not *we*. I try to keep my voice low so that this sounds like average information. "Like I said, there was no reason for you to stick around," I say. "*I* took the dress." I turn to the glass and whisper, "*We* didn't." I watch the snow collect itself into towers that hug the window glass—it accumulates and blocks my view. "And I'll hang on to it," I say.

"What?"

"Not forever."

"Claire—" The librarian reappears. I don't bother looking at him.

"I'm going to get it clean, first," I say quietly. "I want it to be right when it goes back. It has to go back perfect." Outside, Holyoke slides by, out of focus. It could be any snowy town. "I'm sure you agree with that—that it has to be clean and perfect?"

"Claire—"

"It's the responsible thing to do," I say, my voice rising in an overly confident and stupidly cheerful tone. "I just need to figure out how." I manufacture a smile that matches my voice. "Oh, and you know what? I just remembered my father and I have to go somewhere later. I can't stay out long," I say. "So no pizza—but thanks."

There are more things in heaven and earth than are dreamt of in your science class, Horatio. For example, a Girl walks into chemistry, waiting to see Her Friend. If the last time she saw Her Friend she seemed to be wearing Emily Dickinson's clothes, was it a ghost or a madwoman she was seeing?

There's Tess, rounding that corner. Her hair bounces as if she's a girl from a shampoo commercial. She is wearing the peach sweater that makes her skin glow. How to start with Tess? I could start with logic. Probability.

- What is the probability that one small girl would be alone with her mother when her mother tried to kill herself—multiple times?
- What is the probability that she would be the last person to see two people just before they disappeared, and that this trend might continue, involving others?
- What is the probability that if that small girl had done just *one tiny thing* differently—walked faster, arrived on time, hugged more—that things would have changed, that these people—these two people, this mother and this best friend—would have lived for another day? For another year? Forever?

I'll say: *It was one of the worst days of my life.*

But which one to start with?

The beakers are lined up, like a collection, all of their beaks pointed at me, like a glass firing squad—or at least a pecking squad.

There was this strange weather that day, you see, Tess—fog stayed close to the ground, like a stage effect involving a smoke machine. It looked supernatural, but there was science to explain it: the snow melted and the temperature dropped. It happens in that part of Rhode Island in February. It stayed that way all day, with fog close to the ground, not lifting. The trees that seemed to grow from the clouds, cars driving through the clouds. The houses could have been built on top of beanstalks. And among the clouds, at the top of the beanstalks, was a kingdom where everyone was looking for Richy.

After we consider all the data, I'll ask her what she thinks: *What is the probability someone like you would still choose me for a friend?*

The first thing she does is reach out to me with the arms of her peach-colored sweater. Then she covers me all up with a hug.

She smells like oranges and vanilla.

"So tell me," she whispers in my ear, "human or dancer?"

I feel my head tilt. "Hmm?"

"Come on, Little Miss Claire." She leans her bouncing hair closer to me. "Tell me *what you've been doing with Mr. Tate?* But first—" She holds up a finger. "Human or dancer?"

I feel my mouth open.

"Oooooh. It's bad, isn't it?" She's laughing. She pulls a chair close to mine at the lab table. *"Neither human nor dancer?"* She collapses on the chair, and the beakers go *ping*. "I am sooo sorry, my friend. And what about"—she leans closer and whispers so quietly I can almost not hear her, not that I have to hear her say these two words to know they're coming next—"that dress?"

"Oh," I say. "You noticed."

She's grinning and shaking her head at the same time. "Quite a pair, you two. It was on the news, about it being stolen."

I press my eyes closed tightly. "I guess I'll go to jail instead of college," I say. "It won't be that different from high school. And at least I won't be in high school anymore."

"We can't let that happen," she says. "There's enough tragedy in the world." I see her face as she says this. Now she looks sad, all her sparkle extinguished. Or at least most of it.

"What's happened to you?" I say, looking at her carefully. "I know Gus is gone, but did something else happen, too?"

"It's not important. What about the dress? What are you going to do with it?"

"Forget that for now. What's wrong with *you*? Is it Gus?"

Her lips form a straight line. "He brought this present right before he left."

I nod. *This is good. Right?*

"It was a square white box. So what did I do?"

"You screamed?"

"Yeesss. But you won't believe this—I started saying how I loved it, how it was just what I wanted to remember him while he was gone, how it's so perfect—I said, 'I know right where I'll keep this so it catches the sun.'" I can see the creases near her eyes get heavy.

"You said that? You said, 'I know right where I'll keep it'?"

Her face scrunches up. I didn't know a face could scrunch up that much. "It was—it was a *cake*. A chocolate cake."

I hear the ache in her voice. I feel my mouth get dry.

"It wasn't the *cake*. I would have loved the cake. *He baked me a cake. He even went to the bakery and got a box.* It was adorable. *He got an empty box and baked me a cake—a chocolate cake.* It was what came next that was horrible. He knew I thought he was giving me glass. That I was thinking—" Her head drops to the table. I stare at the part in her hair. She says something in a high-pitched voice, too muffled by her hair and arms for me to hear.

"What, Tess?"

Her face pops up quickly. "He said, 'Do you think we're *there* at glass?'" Her lips and cheeks are very red. "What was I supposed to say?"

He's the perfect giant, the one who said, "There's no one in the world like Tess." What else would she say?

"*Yes?*"

That's when the crying starts.

Chapter 12

I KNOW IT'S TESS from blocks away, even though I can see only her face. I know the way she walks like a warrior goddess, surveying her domain. I slow down and drive parallel to her. When she realizes it's me behind the wheel, her eyes get wide and I hear her scream as I open the window.

"You ditched and went to Putney? For *meeeee*?" she squeals. She's practically climbing through the window. "He texted me just now. He's coming home this weekend."

Though the website said there are five hundred scenic acres at the Putney School, and I knew I'd only need to sort through 220 students—56 percent girls, 44 percent boys. It was urgent that I show Tess that I have many sides to my character. It could be important once she discovers that hanging out with me in some towns is considered the equivalent of being friends with a serial killer. Give or take.

Besides, somebody needed to tell him she meant *yes*.

"How did you find him?" She squeezes her whole head, a shoulder, and an arm—all of herself she can—through the window.

I shrug. "Google," I say. That it might seem stalkerlike and out of proportion for me to seek him out at his boarding school didn't occur to me until I was on my way home. Seriously—it could have gone either way.

But what choice did I have?

Someone needed to tell him that he is the perfect giant for her. And that she takes chances—that's one of the things I love most about her. Only this time it was too important, and she stopped short.

What's more important than the truth about how Tess really feels?

It was the cake's fault. Cake shouldn't have the last word.

"It wasn't that hard once I figured out which art building he might be coming out of. He stands out in a crowd," I say.

Initially he did look frightened. I must have had those bulging eyes I get when I have to say something I think is important. But, as someone who comes from a long line of artists and unpredictability, he gave me a chance to prove to him I had no weapons. He even hugged me—not a head hug, either, a real hug.

I said, "Oh, Gus, if we could go back to the Amazing Bean last Saturday—though there's nothing wrong with cake—instead of cake, I'd say: All you need is a token. No box. Something you pull out of your pocket, like—*you* had this and now it's *hers*, and she should *put it someplace so she can see it when she wakes up*. That part's important, Gus, because *it's all in the words*, all in the way you say, 'Put it someplace so you can see it when you wake up.'"

He nodded and he looked at the floor of that very rustic building where we were talking. I could see what he was thinking, that it wasn't an easy question, and that for him the answer was also incomplete.

Are we *there*?

Because who knows if you are *there*? I told him that. I said, "Maybe you are and maybe you aren't, but you won't know if you don't keep going."

He was nodding. *Yes, he was.*

And then I asked him. I said, "If you didn't mean this the way I heard it, I'll understand. But this is what I heard, Gus. You said, 'There's no one in the world like Tess.' *Did you mean that the way it sounded?* Because it sounded pretty great."

I'm looking at her face shoved through the car window, and thinking that there is no one in the world like Tess. "And he said—?"

"Of course he said yes. He said yes, he meant it." I'm looking at the way her face turns a hundred shades of pink when she's excited. But there is also some blue light washing over things now, in waves.

A small crowd of onlookers, I notice, is gathering on the sidewalk behind Tess. I manage a quick glance at what might be causing the attention. There is a police car right behind me, I notice, with its blue flashing lights alarming the townsfolk.

I feel my heart begin to beat hard.

"Tess, step away from the car. Now. NOW." In my side mirror I'm watching the door to the police car behind me as it opens and I'm pressing the button to close the passenger-side window at the same time. I don't seem to be breathing. In fact, other than the finger doing the pressing and my quite active pulse, the rest of me is paralyzed.

"Oww," I hear as I see Tess struggling to get her arm out of the window.

"Oh. No," I whisper. I watch her stumble back from the car. At the same moment, I hear two distinct taps at the driver's-side window. I turn and see the officer's mirrored glasses on the other side.

I'm frozen.

It's muffled, but I know exactly what he's saying.

"Step out of the car, miss."

The street has filled up with people. Tess's bright face bobs just above a sea of dark coats. I'm standing by the back of my father's car, as instructed. My face is burning hot.

The February sun is setting prematurely behind the shops on Pleasant Street. The name of the place is only slightly ironic just now, as my life is changing shape around the edges and the light fails and all I can think is, *I hope they didn't get Tate, too, I hope they didn't get Tate, too, I hope they didn't.*

Two days ago, between classes, an Amherst College professor noticed his car was missing from his usual parking spot. He immediately phoned the police. His car was recovered eight hours later, just blocks from his office.

His daughter, who is now grounded and is serving time in their living room, posing as a girl with homework, was driving.

Apparently, there are several reasons for the police to search a car I might be driving. Who knew? I could have a stolen dress. I could be driving *a stolen car*, too. Intention means nothing when it comes to possession.

It's Sunday, two days after the incident involving the car being reported stolen in a town with almost no crime rate. I'm reading the first line of "The Fall of the House of Usher" for English:

*During the whole of a dull, dark and soundless day in the
autumn of the year when the clouds hung oppressively low
in the heavens . . .*

"It's not just this time," my father is saying in a very modulated
tone of voice. "It's everything since we've moved here."

You have no idea, I'd like to say.

". . . I'm trying to give you your independence, Claire. I've been
trying to give you time, but frankly, it's looking like you have a
penchant for dishonesty."

I think about the word *penchant*, how he says this word rou-
tinely. *You and that penchant of yours.*

"Your lying to the police about that guy who was posing as your
boyfriend is just one small example."

Example of what? My participation in the conversation is op-
tional. My father's face is aimed at a book, but I don't think he's
reading so much as imitating a guy killing time. He's as unfamiliar
with grounding me as I am with being grounded.

An all-purpose lie goes: *Somehow Tate, the student teacher from
English class, wandered into the scene. Accidentally. Coincidentally.*

"Didn't you say he's a student teacher? In which class? And why
did you say you were dating him if he was a student teacher?"

"He *had been* a student teacher. In English. He was finished by
then." I utter random facts, nothing that clears things up. "It was
a story," I say. "One told in a moment of panic. You know? That
kind of story?"

"I've felt that whole explanation was incomplete, but I wanted
to offer you the benefit of trust. Now I see you're developing some

terrible habits around deception. Why did you say he was bloody? What happened to him?"

"He was hit by an oar. He needed some ice," I say. *Wandering around with a likely concussion. I had planned on nursing him back to health, but then I saw the police car.*

I see a lot of police cars. Sometimes it's hard to keep them straight.

"I know you think lying to the police about boyfriends is somehow advantageous, but . . ."

Another lie goes: *I saw the police car and I panicked. I just happened to run into this guy who had been a student teacher (who'd been hit by an oar?). I said he was my boyfriend. It made me seem normal. I was undercover as this rower's girlfriend . . .*

"I'm wondering," I say, only kind of interrupting him, "if I can see Tess. I promise I won't steal anything—" I stop. Why did I say that, why *steal*? Because I stole my father's car. *But why else?* "Or set fires—" (*Now there are fires, too?!*) "Or anything. We'll have some ice cream. Can I get some ice cream with my friend Tess, please, Dad? Please?"

"No." He doesn't even look at me, but he does shake his head. "No more trouble. No more police. No more lies."

"I'm eighteen."

"I know. I've been giving you your privacy, trying to let you work things out, as you asked. You said *let me try*, and I did. I'm a reasonable person. You're going to college in the fall." I listen to the sound of that, how improbable it is that I could actually finish high school. That somehow the whole thing with the dress might work out.

It might.

"But I think you aren't working things out," he says. "You seem to be making things worse. I'm worried about you."

Behind him out the window, the trees seem to shiver in the wind.

I see that in his imagination, come September, we'll load up my things and he'll drop me off on a campus just like his, and he'll join those parents he's been watching all these years, the ones he says never know what to do with their hands—the dads hold keys, the moms hang on to their purse straps like they're the rigging of a ship. They squeeze tightly so that nothing goes off course. *Goodbye,* they say, *be good.*

I need to ask him something. I'd like to ask, "Do you think it's possible to imagine something and then it happens? Does it only work for things you dread—or is it possible—still—for you to *hope* and have *that* thing come true?"

The night she . . . I could start explaining the whole dress thing like that, because it started then. It didn't start on that night last December. I'd get stuck if I tried to explain. I know I would. But if I could force myself, I'd start like this: *That night five years ago— afterwards, it seemed like the house was so empty, like more than one person was gone—didn't it?*

"I promise I'll come back," I say softly instead. I have the same view he does. Out the same window, I can see the trees go back and forth in the wind.

I won't leave you forever, I swear.

He's not moving a bit.

"It was for Tess—that I took the car. I had to find her boyfriend Gus and explain something. It's normal for girls to help each other. *Normal.* Can't you see that what I did is just what you've been hoping for me? That it's the equivalent of wearing pastels?"

"You're saying taking the car to Vermont—without telling me—is like wearing pastels?" I can hear in his voice that something's changing.

"Yes?"

I hear him inhale deeply, and exhale. This takes a full thirty seconds.

"Just ice cream?" I ask.

It's so quiet we can hear the bare branches in the wind scraping against one another. "It's too cold for ice cream anyway," he says. He takes a slow, deep breath. "Have hot chocolate instead."

"So, where'd you find a Get Out of Jail Free card?" She's sitting across the booth from me, her eyes so dark they're almost black. I forget that until I'm with her.

"I told him I needed to help a friend."

"That's all it takes? Your father is easy on felons." She laughs, leans back in the booth.

"It's—" I feel my fingers touch my lips. "He knows it's important when I say I have to help a friend . . . because I haven't had many." I look at the tabletop instead of her. If I look at her, I might stop again. "I never told you about that—about not having many friends . . . There are some other things," I say, "that I haven't told you . . . too."

I look up but beyond her. The movements and colors of the customers at Bart's Ice Cream shop morph in a kaleidoscopic blur behind her. I try hard to focus on getting the story straight. "A while ago I mentioned one friend—my best friend—Richy—about how I lost him?"

"You said he's complicated. I remember."

"Yeah. I said he *was*, remember? He's gone," I say. "What I meant to tell you was that he died."

"Oh, that's terrible. I'm sorry. I should have asked you more about him."

She leans forward, moves her hand across the tabletop toward mine.

"No, I probably wouldn't have—I mean, I've been trying not to tell you . . . much."

I see her head tilt. "Why?"

"I didn't want to . . . be the same person I was before. I wanted a new start, away from all that . . ." I'm trying very hard to keep eye contact. "But I want you to know the whole story now."

"What story?"

"You know my mother—killed herself. You don't know that I found her, and I was alone with her when she tried other times."

I feel her hand on mine. I could stop here, because isn't this enough to try to explain? But I don't. I force myself to go on. "And then Richy disappeared last February."

"Disappeared? I thought you said—"

"We didn't know for a long time—until December—that he died. The last time I saw Richy, we were behind the mall," I say. "There was orange water that always came from the storm drains, and the ducks I decided would be mutant because of the color of the water . . ."

He said he was all gay now and that Jesus wouldn't mind.

I remember asking, "Did Jesus mind when you were part gay?"

"He was starting to do some things that were—well, out of my comfort zone."

117

And out of his, I knew.

I look over at Tess, who is concentrating very hard on my face. She's not just looking at my eyes. She's scanning my whole face, looking at it as if she's seeing the coding underneath, too. Like she's reading my DNA. "I know I'm rambling. It's a long story. Richy was involved with these new things, and I was trying to follow along, but not joining in, you know? He had been my best friend, but I wasn't involved in the new stuff."

I take a breath, forge ahead. "Richy was a really funny kid." I feel myself trying to smile, but the corners of my lips are cracked and dry from all the wind. "A sad and funny kid. It's going to be a year next week," I say.

"Wait, he killed himself, too? Just like your mother?" Her voice has an edge to it.

"That's the thing, Tess. The police said it was maybe an accident. His foot could have gotten tangled in that tow rope." I continue because she ought to know it all. "But nobody knows what he was doing on that dock or even how he got to the water, why he was there. I was supposed to go with him, Tess. He was excited—and a little afraid, you know? There was something inside him that knew it was a bad idea—something he sensed. He wasn't supposed to go alone. I was supposed to be there, too. But I was late."

She's looking at her hand, shaking her head.

"Now you know why I didn't want to talk about it? I figured you would think of me as the Angel of Death." My voice is tired, starting to fade, but I keep going. "I told them about the phone message from the dentist last year. They'd looked at his home computer then, but . . . Nobody knows anything about the dentist. Back then, I think they thought I made it up."

But I didn't. Richy played the message for me. *"I'll see you to-ni-eet."* I won't forget that sound.

"Dentist?" she asks.

It's sickening the way the scent of hot fudge permeates the air at Bart's. Or is it the unearthing of graves that gives me this reaction? A draft of fresh, freezing air from the opening door blows over us.

"It's a long story," I say. "Too much for here, and now."

"Okay," she says. "I get it."

I start to feel relieved, like everything might be okay. "And then there's all this stuff about the dress . . . and Tate . . ."

"Tate?" she asks. "What's he got to do with all this?"

"Uh—" I take a quick breath. "I told him everything—about my mother and Richy and—"

"You *did*?" I feel her hand let go of mine. Her voice is small. It's hurt. The sound of it makes my throat collapse.

"You choose your boys ahead of your girls?" These words make the hairs on my arm rise up.

"I don't have any boys—" I tightly shut my eyes and press my lips together. I use my teeth to hold my lips shut. "It wasn't that way. I didn't *choose* him."

"You told *him*."

I can't look at her for this part. My voice is a little shaky. "You . . . are so happy. It's like an art form with you. I wanted to tell you, but I was afraid I would lose you if you knew about all this. I just didn't want to lose you. It's not just that." I feel myself leaning over, the weight of all this bearing down on my shoulders. "It's like Gus says, 'There's no one in the world like Tess.' I know I'm horrible. I'm an imposter. The more time went by, the more of an imposter I became." I'm bent over so far, my chin is close to the table. "I kept waiting for the right time to tell you who I was—who I really am."

Now the smell of roasting chocolate syrup and the sound of blenders converge into three kinds of sickness. I almost have nothing left to save things. "All I can say is I'm sorry."

I'm watching the table because I can't look at her face.

She lets out a sigh. "Oh, Claire."

"Take some time—don't decide today—if you hate me. Don't decide today, please?"

Two hands crawl over the tabletop. I feel both of them on mine. She squeezes tightly, so tightly I think nothing could make her let go. "You," she says, "are my best friend. You know that?"

This is right before my eyes cloud over and get hot. *Best friend?*

"Why?" I hear my small voice.

"Who went to Putney for me? Who nearly got arrested doing it? Who always makes me laugh?"

"Your best friend was *wanted* in Rhode Island." It's a good thing I can't see the other people eating ice cream, how they might be looking at me. "In addition, your best friend has a stolen dress in her closet and no idea how to fix it, how to get it back where it belongs."

"My best friend is brilliant. My best friend is a legend. Somebody should write a song about her." She squeezes my hand. "But I'm still trying to figure all this out. How did you get the dress?"

I let out a long breath. "That question will take longer. For a while, I'd been getting into the house."

"Getting in?"

"Well . . . *going there.* I never planned on taking anything. I just like how I feel when I'm there. It's not like any other place. That part I can't explain." I shake my head.

"You don't have to," she says. She gives my hands an extra squeeze. "But how is Tate connected to the dress? How did you end up wearing it in the first place? Because it looked like the two of you—"

"Stop," I say. "It's not that way. None of this is. I was at the Amazing Bean that night and he had read my things and thought I was suicidal or homicidal—I'm not sure which, maybe both— and I thought he was telling me that he was conspiring with Per-zan. And I ran out." I can still feel my hot face and the cold air that night, how it was clean and clear like snow. Air like that could heal you from the inside out. "He said I wanted him to follow me." I shake my head. "I know you're thinking I *did* want him to follow me. Maybe that's what his problem is—that he thinks I have a big crush on him. He wanted me to make sure to tell you why we were *together*. That it wasn't . . . well . . . anything. It isn't."

She laughs.

"What? Why are you laughing, Tess? He's never ever going to be my boyfriend or anything. Why would I crave attention like that? What would that say about me? That I'm chasing around a guy I don't know the first thing about."

She leans way back in the booth and rolls her eyes up to the ceiling dramatically. "Let's be honest, Claire. Why *wouldn't* you want him to follow you? I think a better question"—she raises her eyebrows—"is, *Why did he?*"

Chapter 13

AT THE JONES LIBRARY in Amherst, there's a collection of Emily Dickinson's letters. This week I have spent hours staring at her handwriting. I know it's idolatry that it does not matter what the words say, just that Emily Dickinson's pen made these shapes, that Emily Dickinson's hand folded this paper, that when I walk by her letter, I feel its light. The same feeling comes from my bedroom closet.

When I open my e-mail, I see the message line: Richy DiMarco Memorial Service Sunday.

I type furiously, my fingertips hitting the keyboard hard. *Richy DiMarco.* For the first time, I visit his Internet grave. There's just part of his face in the artful picture, one eye and a piece of wing.

Hello old/odd friend.

I feel something stone press into the center of my chest.

I reach my hand up to where my heart might be.

I vowed I would not go looking for your picture,
except every now and then I do accidentally

happen to see the two of us appear
in brochures that come from the colleges we decided
would be nothing like our high school.
In the one that came today, it's autumn, of course
and we are sitting
under a radioactive tree, eating Goldfish crackers.
We seem to love books and are happy
in our afterlife.

Then I hear something that ends in "car?" It's not until the last word that I recognize the voice.

I look behind me. It's Tate, his hair swept back off his face as if the weather had attempted a makeover.

I see Tate's eyes—it's easy to be surprised by that shade of green—but I also notice his face is full of drama. An orchestra could indicate the mood of it. There would be cymbals, drums.

"Tate? How did you know I was—"

"You were driving a stolen car?" He's angry.

"Well, it was my *father's* car. Not quite *stolen*. I just forgot to ask," I say. "How do you—know about it?"

"Claire, it's a small campus. When a car gets stolen, people hear about it. And when the story has a punch line, the story gets around even faster."

He puts his hand on the arm of my swivel chair as he leans over. He drops his head and his voice gets lower. "You have that dress hanging in your closet and *you're stealing cars?*" It's a whisper that shouts.

"It's okay," I say, holding up the palm of my hand. "I had to fix

things—before I told Tess. It turned out fine. Except I got grounded."
I smile. "Anyway, I told her everything."

He's frowning. His skin is red, chapped.

"I'm taking care of the situation."

"What do you mean, you're taking care of it? You're taking care of things by getting more attention from the police? Is that how you're taking care of it?"

"Why are you so"—I shake my head—"angry? You said it yourself. You're glad to walk away from this. You're not in English class anymore, so I don't see you, and I'm taking care of it. And how did you know where I was?"

"I see you all the time, Claire. It's a small town."

All the time?

"I—I don't think we should be talking about this *here*." I motion with my head.

Tate looks behind him. No one is there. In fact, except for him and me, the room is empty. His forehead wrinkles up. "Huh?"

I motion with my chin to the glass case on the wall behind him, where I can see what looks like ordinary paper but what is actually one of Emily Dickinson's letters. "Not *here*."

He rolls his eyes. "I have to leave now. I'm finishing a huge paper that's due tomorrow," he says. "But I'd like to talk to you about this some more. Are you still grounded?"

"Uh, no. Turns out neither my father nor I am very good at it."

"Okay, tomorrow, after the library."

Chapter 14

"I SAW WHAT YOU MEANT about the bird's wing the other day,"
Tate says.

I'm walking down the street normally, my father would be
glad to know. No detours or head-fakes. Just a stroll down Pleasant Street to the Amazing Bean with the guy who helped me
steal Emily Dickinson's dress. And in the sixty seconds or so this
has been happening, I haven't drawn blood. It's all good.

"Hmmm?"

"That was Richy in the picture, right? On your laptop—at the
library. I saw the name. I figured."

"Yes. Today's the day," I say. I press my eyes closed. I shove my
fist into my coat pocket, where it mashes into some coins and strains
the seam.

He's quiet. "What day?" he asks softly.

"One year ago today. The day he was, you know, whatever. The
last—time I saw him." My voice gives up.

We walk for a while in silence. Just our footsteps amplified on the wet sidewalk make any noise.

"His father came to get revenge, you know? Later." I start to laugh, but I stop myself.

"Why?" Tate asks.

"Because I was the last one to see him. Because I wore black, and my mother—because I was a goth girl."

"He knocked on the door and said, 'I'm going to kill you'?"

"Not quite. I didn't know why he was there at first. I just happened to look out the window. I remember seeing him on his knees, on our front lawn in his parka. I thought he was praying out there. It wouldn't have seemed odd, to pray at a time like that, but it was a strange place to do it. And I remember he was doing something with his arms. I was upstairs in my room, at the window. I had to keep clearing the glass with my sleeve to see."

I find myself stopping under a streetlight.

"My father must have seen him, too, because he entered the frame. He was wearing his bedroom slippers on the snow. All of a sudden, Richy's father scrambled up to his feet and charged at him. His hands were straight in front, heading right for my father's chest." I demonstrate. I see my shadow arms in the streetlight doing the same.

"I heard yelling, but I couldn't make out the words. Richy's father was not saying the prodigal had returned, that was for sure," I say.

"And then this thing happened—my father pivoted at his hips, his top half going in one direction and his bottom half stuck going the other way. His feet were slipping into no particular positions on the melting ice. It was just like watching a cartoon escape—but it wasn't funny. It was terrifying."

"Like one of those horror cartoons?" he says. I can't see his face. If he's smiling, it's just for a second before he gets serious again. I hear it in his voice. "I think I know what you mean now."

"The sound was the horror—it was the worst part of the whole thing. The door slamming first, and then his father started this banging. It was almost like music, like some kind of sad music." I slap my fist on my hand. "Boom—pause—boom—pause—boom. It was like he was in complete control and coming to get me. It was so *eerie*." I pause for a breath. "First my father yelled, 'Call the police.' The house was shaking."

I notice my shadow from the streetlight.

"And then I heard the crash. It was like part of my brain was exploding, too. And my father was yelling, 'Lock your door, Claire. Lock your door.' Can you imagine it—the guy banging the door down?" I find myself out of breath, like I've run the whole way here, instead of stopping under the light.

I take a full minute to watch the way the wet street shimmers in the blue light. Tate's shadow seems far away from mine, and smaller.

"But that wasn't the day Richy disappeared," I say, starting to walk again. "Richy's father didn't come to get me until weeks later. Until it seemed hopeless. The day Richy disappeared—from all that fog on the ground, it was like we were up in the clouds, like a fairy tale. A bad one. Is it eight yet?"

"It's seven thirty," he says quietly.

"Seven thirty. He was still alive then. So one year ago at this exact time, Richy was alive." I hear my voice crack on the last two words. "He sent me a text that said he couldn't wait. I guess he didn't have much time . . ."

"Or maybe he knew you would try to stop him—?"

"Oh. Does that matter? He's gone and no one knows why. But—it's got to be there—some kind of clue about what happened. It's got to be there somewhere."

"Claire . . ." he says. "You told the police all you know. You've done all you can."

I turn. "Huh?"

"There's something in your voice. The way you're talking. It's like the night we ended up with that dress. I know it's a bad day, but what are you—?"

I puff out a cloud of breath into the cold air and watch how fast it disappears.

"What are you thinking about *doing*?" he says.

"I'm not thinking about doing anything." I turn back and walk quickly ahead of him, but then pivot on my heel and face in his direction. "But there's this part that doesn't make sense. If he met the dentist over the Internet, like he said, why couldn't they find anything on his computer? Why no phone record? I heard the call. If I could just figure *that* out."

"Can you get some coffee, or do you have curfew? I need to give you something."

In the Amazing Bean they're playing Bob Dylan.

"It's weird how they say your family survived."

"Hmmm?" He looks up at me.

"In obituaries. They say you, the dead person, are survived by . . . Like all the rest of us managed to escape somehow."

He's looking down.

"I'm sorry," I say. *For being me.*

"*I'm* sorry it's such a bad day."

"It's a bad day, yes. A bad year, too—a bad couple of years? My life is complicated and never seems to get any simpler." Bob Dylan is there, singing backup to this scene. I look at Tate, who now seems to have contracted my sorrow. I'd like to change that. I really would.

"I know I control some of it, and some of it I don't. And I'm trying to figure out which is which. I'm also," I say, with something I hope sounds like authentic optimism, "trying to come up with a way to get the dress repaired. I think I have a plan."

Tate rolls his eyes. "That's what I was afraid of." He looks off. He exhales. I see him reach into the pocket of his puffy down vest. He roots around for a while and comes up with a pen and a small notebook.

"You have a notebook in there?"

"Uhm-hmm. I bring it everywhere."

"So, you're rowing down the Connecticut, and all of a sudden— Note to Self?"

He looks up, his eyes squinting.

I see him flip to an empty page in the back and write something. "You have really simple ideas about other people. You know that?"

I feel my face heat up.

"I write down things I see—or read—anything that I wouldn't want to forget." He tears out a sheet and I watch him flip through some pages. He stops. "'There's a reason they call it deadweight,'" he reads.

I swallow.

"'You already know about the heaviness of dead things—but

today lifting this one bird—all you can think about' "—he stops and looks at me—" 'is air.' "

Oh.

His fingers drag a sheet of that small notebook paper across the table. "It's not hard to remember, but I've written it down anyway," he says. "It's 'state at Amherst dot e-d-u.' I forget to charge my phone, so that's almost always useless, but I check this all the time. Now you can get in touch whenever you need to do something illegal. We have a dress to return, and we have to figure out how to get it cleaned. You can't go to jail for a different crime before we do that."

Am I able to breathe yet? "State?" I manage to ask.

"The first letter of my name plus Tate. Pretty basic."

"Wh-what *is* your name?"

I hear him chuckle. "Sam. As in Sam I Am." His eyes focus on something past me, and his face all of a sudden goes blank. "Uh-oh."

"What's wrong?"

"Your father—"

"He's at a lecture. About tombs. Egyptian, I think. It's that professor he's been working with—"

"He's not at the lecture anymore." I see Tate put on some kind of imitation look of delight. "He's heading over here."

"I thought that was you over here."

I turn and look up. It's my father all right, looking very nice in his dark overcoat and scarf. Looking understatedly puzzled— nearly placid, in fact. Tate's chair scrapes across the floor as he reaches out to shake hands with him, saying, "It's nice to see you again."

I hear my father say, "You're looking better than the last time. Your nose healed well. Those injuries can be tricky." I watch my father, who now seems like a person I only sort of know, turn to a woman, I now notice, who is by his side. She's in a dark coat, too, with a violet scarf peeking out over the collar. "A terrible rowing accident. Did you know crew was so rough?" he asks her.

Tate shoots me a look.

"This is Grace Lonaghan. She's the Smith professor I'm collaborating with. It was her lecture tonight." The new man, who only resembles my father, looks over at her and smiles. "She was fantastic."

I see Tate raise his eyebrows a tiny bit. It's a subtle thing, but I catch it.

"Hello," he says, reaching over to shake Grace's hand. "Was there a good crowd?"

Was there a good crowd? Two points, Tate.

"Oh, yes," my dad says, nodding enthusiastically. "Packed the room."

"It was a very small room," Grace says, laughing. She turns to me then. "Your father has told me so much about you. It's good to meet you finally."

Finally? "Uh huh. Yes. You, too. He mentioned you're—an Egypt expert—right?"

He forgot the *very-attractive-woman* part.

"Oh, he always overstates." She bats at his coat sleeve with her hand, which I note is covered in a purple leather glove. He looks at the floor in some kind of trance. Is my new dad blushing? I can't stop looking at his face.

"Your work is at the front of . . ." He starts a long protest that seems like a letter of recommendation.

I am distracted by something that hits my foot. I feel it again, harder. I look down. It's Tate's foot tapping mine. I look over. He does something with his mouth.

Huh?

I watch him raise his finger to his chin and move his mouth shut.

Oh. My mouth is quite open—as in wide open. I ease it closed and casually run my fingers through my hair.

When my father finishes talking, Tate says, "So sorry to be running. We were just leaving."

My father suddenly has forgotten our new friend, Grace, and is now very interested in Tate. In fact, he's really studying that guy's face.

"Homework," I say.

"I don't believe we were ever introduced that day." A more familiar version of my dad slowly extends his hand toward Tate but shifts his stare over to me.

"Right. Well, this is Tate—"

"Sam Tate," he says, vigorously shaking my father's hand. "It wasn't the opportune moment, that's for sure, Professor Salter."

The handshake seems to be taking a long time.

I clear my throat. "Nice to meet you—Grace."

"I'll be home soon," my dad says. He's looking at Tate.

Outside, in the shadows of the shops, I watch Tate press his eyes shut. It's very dark, but the gesture still says a lot. "Rowing accident?"

"Sorry," I say. "I didn't think the two of you would ever meet again."

"We live in *Amherst*," he says. "He teaches at *my college*."

"It's fine," I say. "After the dress is all settled—"

"Settled? We don't even have a plan—"

"My plan," I say, "is to go out of town—maybe Boston or something—and find someone who restores antiques."

"People who deal with antiques but don't know this dress is missing? It was on the news."

I feel my face wrinkle up.

"Not a great plan," he says. "And a *rowing accident*? I thought you were going to stop lying?"

Even though it's very dark where we are standing, I try to see his face. "I haven't ever lied—*to you*." I try hard to find a good connection to his eyes in the bad light. "You believe me, don't you? *That I have never lied to you?*"

I hear a thump. I seem to have backed him into a brick wall. "I do," he says. "But you have to promise me you won't start. And this is important—*you have to mean it*."

Chapter 15

"THAT MAN BEAT OUR DOOR DOWN." This is my father speaking with great authority about why I can't go to Richy's memorial service. "It's absolutely not safe. No." He is using a good deal of body language to express his inner thoughts. His arms are tightly wound around his seated body. He seems to be made of wire.

"He didn't have—" I stop to touch my fingers to my lips. I must do this because what I am about to say shouldn't be true. Is this a learned gesture or something we figure out in the womb—how, automatically, a hand goes to the mouth that's going to say something unbearable?

I move my fingers and quietly I finish. "Any other friends. *I was it.*"

I was.

And he was mine.

We had each other.

We were stretched out on Richy's bed, looking at brains. The room was full of them—infrared scans and line diagrams taped up on the wood-paneled walls. There was a boxed picture on sheets of cellophane showing different layers. And models. One of them was motorized, on a revolving platform. If you closed your eyes you could always hear the pulse of it, whizzing around.

"This is the part that's gay," he says, "or not." He points with his toe to the red part of one of the fluorescent scans.

It was his theory about how the brain is a map of your life, all of your choices in there, just waiting for you to make them.

"So it's all set up for you ahead of time?" I ask. "If that's a fact, I'd like a rewrite. Script girl?!"

"I mean, you hope not," he says, drifting off. "It's not set in stone for us yet. Our brains are still gooey. But soon."

What was to come was waiting to happen?

I could hear his dog downstairs in a barking contest with the neighbors' dogs. The window was open and a breeze carried the sound of the guard dogs' heavy chains colliding with the metal fence. Every once in a while, the chains hit the fence hard, like waves crashing on shore.

"The thing is, you never know about your brain," he said. "I mean, you can read your palm. But to read your brain you have to be—you know?"

He always left out the "dead." He was sensitive about my situation, the fresh wounds and all. He might have preferred "called back," but now I'll never know.

"Do they keep you up at night?" I changed the subject to dogs. "They are so—growly."

"I'm usually up drawing then anyway," he said. "Because for me creativity always works the night shift." Papers spilled off a folding table *stuffed into the tiny room near the bed. I could see many drawings of boots—black, with blocky heels, and zippers with sharp silver teeth.*

"Those are big zippers," I said.

"Women love big zippers," he said, smiling.

"Which part of the brain determines that?" I asked.

"The part that says you're a girl," he said, "but not only females have that."

"So . . ." I look over at my dad. It looks uncomfortable having a wire body. "So . . . ," I say, "Grace."

The wire seems to change position once it seems I have given up on the memorial service.

"She's very pretty," I say.

Even more shifting of wires. It's slight, but significant.

"She's my partner—" he says. "My *research* partner." Chair springs squeak and joints become activated: one elbow bends and one hand rests on a knee; the other elbow perches on the arm of the chair.

"Why didn't you—"

Oops, his hands come together in a protective reflex, fingers clasping each other tightly.

"She seems interesting," I try again. "We should have her over."

His hands, conjoined, slowly move to under his chin. The chin settles on the ledge they form. "You wouldn't mind."

I know it's a question, even though it doesn't sound like one. But I understand. It's something he needs to be certain about. "In fact, you should cook for her," I say. "Does she like pork chops?"

Is he smiling? I can't tell. I've got something else on my mind. I'm thinking of the kind of memorial service that Richy and I might have planned. We should have prepared better. It would have to be a private service, we would have understood, with just one—or the other—survivor.

Up in my room I open my laptop.

TO: state@amherst.edu

First, I'm only writing b/c you said you wanted me to tell you, but
according to the law, does it count as stealing the car
if I get permission to take it one place but then go someplace else?
And does it matter if I'm crossing state lines?

Chapter 16

"IT'S STAYING LIGHT LONGER. You notice it in late February," Tate says. The clouds look like canyon-rock layers as the sun sets, a giant wall of orange and slate.

We are sitting in Tate's car, which he has parked across from the church where Richy's memorial service is about to start. He insisted I not take my father's car across state lines.

"So," I hear him say.

I hear him shifting in his seat.

He makes some kind of noise. He's humming two notes. I watch his fingers tracing the steering wheel as he does this. They start moving like he's playing piano.

"We'll be on the river soon," he says. His fingers play piano faster. "And off the ergs. The indoor part of rowing—on the machines—is definitely not my favorite." His piano playing picks up. "Yep . . . The first day on the water makes it all worth it." Now I hear a light drumming, his whole hand bouncing off the steering wheel. "I'll miss that next year." I watch as the drumming joins the piano playing. "Yes, I will . . . Rowing? Am I still talking about rowing?"

I turn to the church. The dark colors of the windows illuminate slowly as the sunlight fails, and the windows take on a different life. Inside there, they will be saying something about Richy. They'll be trying to make sense.

I should be there, too.

Then the car is silent. No drumming, no soundless piano.

Then I hear him cough. "Don't you want to make a snappy remark about rowing?" he says.

"What?"

"I'm just trying to get you to say something back. What's going through your mind? Whatever you're thinking of spontaneously doing—I'd like to get a heads-up. Before you—you know—jump out of the car or something. Could you warn me, please? I know it would have been worse if you'd come by yourself. I'm trying to figure out what you are thinking about."

I look at my hands.

"Maybe we shouldn't have come," he says. "Just being here nearby—and your not going in—that was our bargain, but maybe that wasn't a good idea."

I look over at him. "I can't say it didn't cross my mind to say the deal's off and run in." I shake my head. "Is this—what's going on in there—is it supposed to end things? For it to be over afterward?"

"I know this is hard, being here and not being able to go inside. I think your father is right, though. What if that guy decides to go after you again?"

"It wasn't the way it sounds. Richy's mother came—to explain."

She stood in the shattered doorway of our house. She was leaning on one broken side as if she had been propped up like a Halloween scare-crow. It seemed possible a wind might tip her.

She said, "No, I won't come in. I should not be here." Her eyes did not find mine.

"She told me he'd been drinking. That's how she explained it."

"He heard you might have . . ." Richy's mother's voice got very tiny.

I nodded. I did not say this, but it made sense about me and the implication of doom. My mother first, so now Richy.

"Richy probably told you about him."

I shrugged. We didn't talk much about our families. "Richy just told me his father had a lot of opinions." He had actually said very little about his father. He had told me more about their dog. The dog's idea of being house-trained, Richy had said, was to pee next to the toilet. He had said the whole family liked Taco Thursdays because the taco shells made so much noise it took the place of talking.

"Richy's father did—" She flinched as if something had flown into her face. "Does not like Richy staying out late," she said sadly. She stopped and seemed to think about that for a while. Then she looked up. Her eyes were shiny, deeply black. "You aren't to blame," she said. She lifted her hand to put a finger under my chin. "I know you don't know anything about it."

I exhaled, relieved. But her hand was not leaving my chin. "Do you?" she still had to ask.

"She said she didn't believe them, but, Tate, there were rumors about me. You know?" I can feel my eyes start to bulge. It's a good thing the car is dark. "That's why his father was there. That's who they thought I was. Why I can't go in there—*to my friend's funeral.* It's who I am, still."

I watch his hand reach out toward me. "Here, maybe. But not

everywhere. *And not forever.* Not everyone thinks of you that way. You have—" He stops. His hand is frozen there, in the space between us. "Tess. Right? She'd never think that way about you."

I feel my eyes burning. I close them tightly, but it doesn't seem to help.

I hear Tate take a deep breath. "I have an idea," he says. "Where's a place you would go with him?"

"Wh-what?"

"What *is* a memorial service anyway?"

"O-okay," I say, clearing my throat. "But if we're going to do it right, first we'll have to stop for Goldfish."

He starts up the car.

"And Orangina."

The animals, this far away from being fed, are almost silent. "You can tell they're there even though you don't hear them, you know? Can't you feel them?"

We are in the parking lot outside the Roger Williams Park Zoo just after dusk. The moonless dark covers up almost everything. Some of the night birds that stay all winter are stirring. "Can you feel them breathing? I think animals breathe differently from humans, like air is more important to them."

"So you'd come here and listen to the animals breathing?"

I laugh. "No. But we came here a lot. We could pretend we weren't in our lives anymore. That we were someplace else. I know that sounds pathetic." I look out at the looming dark trees, which don't seem as much like monsters tonight, even though they should. "But it wasn't." I hear myself sigh.

"You said he would sometimes hurt himself?"

"Not like you think. He would do things—like he found out this musician in England with the same name as his carved words into his forearm. Right there."

We are parked under a streetlight, so he can see me lift up my sleeve to show him. "And so Richy did the same." I use my finger to draw the number 4 and the word *ever* across my arm. "4-ever."

"What did it mean?"

"I don't know. Forever what? He didn't know. That's what I'm saying. He was doing things to be on an edge, you know. Maybe it was hurting, but at least it felt like something? I don't know. Do you need a reason to do stupid things, or is having no reason what makes them stupid?"

Tate shakes his head.

"He started to get interested in music. He thought he was going to join a band or something. He was looking for—*an audience*— you know? Any kind of attention. He only barely played guitar. He was really terrible." I feel the bumpy texture of the Orangina bottle.

"He was sad by nature, but he was trying to find—" I stop to think about how to say it. "He was trying to find his way." I listen for the animals for a second. "He wasn't giving up."

I look at Tate. I can see just the outlines of him—whatever the streetlight can find—leaning his head on his hand, his elbow propped up by the steering wheel.

I take a deep breath. It still smells a little like camping in his car, and like grass and mint. It's funny how the scent of that is familiar now, like I could re-create the blend of it and be back here in the dark and in Providence—and yet be warm and not afraid—again, in a memory of this night.

I think Richy would have liked that.

"How's your Orangina?" Tate asks.

"Good," I say. "Thanks. I really mean that. Thanks for driving me so I wouldn't have to steal—well, kind of steal—my dad's car again. And . . . it's okay now." I nod even though he might not be able to see it.

"What is?"

"To ask me about her dress. I know you were letting me have a break from it because of all this. And now it's okay to ask if I've come up with any new ideas. I know you want to ask. Or to tell me what you've thought of. It's okay now."

"I know it is," he says. "But not tonight. It's Richy's turn tonight."

"Then, can I ask your opinion about something else?"

"Sure."

"Do you think it's okay . . . to say goodbye if I don't know what happened to him?"

He exhales. "I don't know. That's for you to decide. But I do know that you can't feel bad because you're the one who's alive."

"How did you know that's—"

He stops doing everything. "Eh—it's . . ." I hear the sound the fabric of his puffy vest makes as he shoves his hands into the pockets. "It's a long story. Not tonight." I hear the clink of keys as he gets ready to start the car. I hear him click his seatbelt.

"Okay," I say quietly. "Another time?"

"I don't know—but probably not," he says. "Sorry."

Oh. "Okay."

"Anyway, what are you telling your father about tonight?"

"I'm not sure he'll notice I've been out. He's pretty busy." I laugh. "With his research partner and all."

Chapter 17

AND NOW THERE ARE NEW SMELLS in our house—the spices of Moroccan food—in the air, even days after the meal. The light is different in my bedroom, too. Is this what March looks like in this house, like it glows? I close my eyes and inhale, and I seem to be in a new house, someone else's house.

My father is not reading. He's looking out the window. Probably because Grace is elsewhere, baking bread for him. Perhaps she is even milling the wheat by ancient Mayan methods. Fun fact: She makes her own coffee mugs and dishes. Maybe she collects the clay from the neighboring riverbed.

"The birds are coming back," he says. He's imagining, probably, the way she touches his cheek. She does this often, even when I am in the room.

I accidentally stepped into the kitchen last Sunday. *Moroccan food smells like cologne,* I was about to say. But then I saw he was reaching his arm around Grace's waist while she tossed vegetables in the pan. I blinked and tried hard to remember my mother cooking with my father—the two of them with nothing bad having just happened, and nothing bad on the way.

I tried.

What I came up with was one day when my mom was making plans for the summer. We were going to go to Maine for two weeks. There was a house she knew about, she was telling us. *She was leaning her head back and looking up, at something ahead that was good. She was seeing a house on a cliff by the ocean.*

There was a window behind her and a sky full of winter. There were gray clouds in that window. She was leaning her head against the glass. She closed her eyes when she talked about the summer and it didn't matter about the gray clouds. I could see summer.

Was she wearing her hair pulled back or was it down?

I force myself to keep my eyes open.

I shut my eyes tight.

I try to remember.

The fact is that I'm losing her more each day. The sound of her voice. How she would smile. *Tell me a story about her,* I could say to him. *Tell me about what I might have already forgotten.* "The birds will freeze. Or starve," I say instead. "It's too early."

"Don't be silly. It's nature. Instinct. They watch for the cues." His voice sounds elsewhere. He's only sort of talking to me. I see it's the wrong time to ask him to remember. "I need to do some homework," I say.

I head upstairs and close my door. I hear he has turned on music. It's that jazz he's been listening to lately. I take my mother's books from the box. I remind myself these were things she loved. I say, *There were parts of your life that were happy.*

I line the books up in a stack in front of the closet door. As I do this, they form a force field. They will protect the dress from invaders.

I do hear some birds outside, but I believe they are the winter type. The kind you know have stayed.

I stare at the blank walls of my room. An empty room with blank walls: That would be the right monument for me. An accurate record of my invisibility. My legacy.

> *Blank walls, the color of butter,*
> *like mine. Somebody is painting*
> *this picture of you: a room*
> *without people or even a chair.*

So that's what I've amounted to?

I take out my laptop and visit Richy, who is seventeen forever on what is now his online memorial. A page with his face, from his past. "I won't forget you," I say, "either." I type *Internet* and *dentist* and then I reverse it. *Dentist* and *Internet*. I hear the whine of small dental tools coming from an instructional video on a website. It's a high, hopeless sound.

I feel myself rubbing my eyes, which are blurry. I type *state@ amherst.edu*. I wait for a minute before I start the message—I really do try to stop myself.

I say that I am thinking it had something to do with the new part of him—the music, the reason he died. I write, *That was the new part, where he got into trouble, where it started to change—he was going to be a musician in his next life.*

Chapter 18

"So why don't you e-mail him?" Tess asks. It's one of those long, misleading rainy days that wash all signs of winter away.

"Who?" I ask, but I know exactly what she's talking about. She's talking about why she's the only one eating the pizza. I'm looking out the window at the parking lot, where people are walking like hunchbacks because of the rain. As if posture had something to do with staying dry.

"It's not him." I am thinking about how the word *insincere* is similar to *not true*. Not quite a lie, but nowhere near *what you really mean*. I'm thinking about Tate saying *I check it all the time*. "It's Richy," I say. "I keep thinking about where he was going that night. I keep going over it . . . He wasn't sure about it. He was taking me along. He'd never done that before. And I was late."

He was wearing his new leather jacket earlier that day. I remember thinking that he would be cold at night. My hands were cold when we were standing there, watching the ducks in the orange water. The ice was like broken glass. The dentist's voice sounded like a bird.

"I hate dentists," I say.

"So why that day? What was different?"

"I don't know. Intuition? He'd traded his high-tops for Italian loafers, but he was still the kid who got put into the locker."

The week before I was his cover. He told his mother he was coming over to my house. He even asked me to meet him there so she could see he was with me.

I was in the kitchen. His mother was a small woman who seemed sewn to a kitchen chair that wheeled. She opened the fridge and got out celery. She pulled over the plastic cutting board. She wielded a large knife. All of this without leaving her chair.

Richy came through the door freshly shirted, patting his bird's wing over his eye.

"Claire's staying for spaghetti," his mother announced.

He smiled at me. Thanks, he mouthed.

Later I asked him where he was headed. He smiled. He said he might be trying some open mic nights, joining a band. That's where he was headed: he was changing direction. I was already missing him. Even before he was really *gone*, when he was just *going somewhere new.*

"Why he's—*gone*—it had something to do with music, I think. I heard the message. He played it for me—from the dentist. It had to do with him and music and a dentist . . . I can't figure out how those things come together.

"The thing is, he asked for my help that night. The last night."

"Claire, don't take this the wrong way."

I look at her over the cold food.

"Why don't you e-mail him? Ask him if he's still alive," Tess says, lifting her drink so the ice crashes around in the cup.

For a second I'm confused.

"I mean Tate," she says. "Hey, Tate, are you still living or did your affiliation with me kill you? Please let me know at your earliest convenience. Love, Claire."

I look at her.

"Okay, just 'Claire.'" She raises her eyebrows. "No 'love.'"

I sigh.

She shakes her head. "Claire . . ." Her voice is soft. "Richy. He's gone. You aren't to blame."

I let go of a deep breath.

"Open your eyes. You need to see the people in your life right now." She smiles with her whole face. She wants me to smile back.

"I see you," I say. "I'm happy to see you."

She laughs. "And no one else?"

I look at her. "What?"

"*I* see that thing you have with him. That connection."

"No, you're wrong. It's nothing."

"You told him everything," she says, "*first.*"

"Tess, it wasn't like that. I was afraid to lose you. I knew I didn't have that to worry about with him—he was just reading my writing, asking me questions because of my writing. That's all."

I hear her exhale slowly. She tilts her head and her black curls sway.

"And when did it change?"

I swallow.

"It wasn't the dress *or* the nose, was it?"

I press my eyes shut.

"You have more hope in you than you know," she says. "You always have."

I feel my face heat up slowly. I hear myself exhale. "I did—I e-mailed him. Last week. He never—wrote back. It doesn't matter. You can't lose something you never had, right? I'll take care of the dress. I can do it."

The colleges have been on spring break, so Grace has been at our house every night. Tonight, I was the tourist and they were the natives, talking about silk in their native language. Grace was holding her fingers together in the air. It was like he could see it there, in her hand. Like he could feel not just that it was soft, but that it was *Chinese* silk, a special kind, and it's like touching clouds.

I said I had homework and so now I am back in my habitat, the blank walls and my mother's books forming a fortress that protects Emily Dickinson's dress. From here, I can hear Grace's laughter downstairs, the way it bubbles alongside his.

When I hear the music start downstairs, and smell the after-dinner coffee, I realize it's going to be a long night. I wish I were sleepy.

I open my e-mail. It's the way heart attacks happen. In just a split second.

> *SUBJECT: I have to see you.*
> *FROM: state@amherst.edu*

When my heart starts up again, it beats hard. *You have more hope in you than you know,* Tess said. I wait for a minute—as long as I can—before I press REPLY. *Okay. Library. 3 p.m. tomorrow?*

Chapter 19

"NICE TAN," I SAY. We are in the lounge at the library and Tate's got that surfer look going again, his hair a shade lighter and his face rosy and golden. And then there's me with my gray sweater, blending into the sky. My layers of coats and scarves, dangling. If you look at him, you say winter is already gone, and at me, you say it will never, ever go.

"I'm sorry I lost you for a bit—your e-mail," he says. "It's not that I didn't want—I mean—we were on the road training in Florida for spring break, and then rowing at a tournament, and it got lost in the queue with hundreds of others. It's been a crazy time."

There is enough motion to make me less visible in the room, more likely to blend in with the institutional furniture. To be invisible.

"Sure." I wave my hand through the air. The word *hundreds*, for some reason, lingers in the air. *Lost among hundreds.* "It wasn't anything. I was bored. My father's *friend* is at the house all the time." I try not to look at him, try hard not to notice the new things that have happened to his face since the last time I saw him, signs of sunlight and wind.

"Anyway, I was thinking—about Richy. I couldn't wait to show you." His voice is full of something. I'm not sure what.

"We were at Brown yesterday," he says. "I picked up some things in Providence. I looked through them really well, and I found this." It's a small newspaper. "You mentioned that Richy was meeting up with a dentist, but that didn't help much. And then I was thinking about music—you know, at our memorial service you said he was trying to break into music."

Our?

"It's a listing of entertainment in Providence."

I watch him turning the pages, his face burrowed into them. While he does this he says something about my e-mail.

"It wasn't important," I say. "I know you're busy, friends, girl-friend, summer job." I'm mumbling, I realize. I wonder if we could talk about something other than death.

Could we?

"You're on the river now, right?" I say. I saw a boat there, two weeks before, a long line of rowers moving in one smooth motion. I was trying to tell which one was him. "I—um—thought I saw your boat." That V the boat's wake made. I was thinking about what he had said about his first day back on the water. How the first day makes the winter worthwhile. I'd like to hear more about that. "It reminded me of the way it looks when ducks land on the surface of the water, but magnified across the whole river. I couldn't tell if it was yours for sure."

I wait for him to say something about that, to tell me anything about himself. Instead I hear papers rattle.

"The river was so still except for the boat. That must be nice," I say.

"It's this . . ." He opens the paper and points to an ad. "It might be nothing, but I couldn't wait to show you. There's a place just outside of Providence, where they have open mic night every Friday. Look." He points. "It's some kind of joke Zen name. Like you get inner peace and Wi-Fi at the same coffee place."

The Innernet.

"It's a long shot, I know, but I thought there was something odd in the way you said he met the dentist *over* the Internet. I mean, most people say *on the Internet*—or *online*—not *over the Internet*. What if he meant over *at* the *Innernet*?"

"*Over at* the Innernet? I don't know . . ."

"Maybe we should mention this place to the police. You know, tell them about this place?"

"Police? No," I say, trying to balance these two moments—the one where he's taking me back to the past, and the one where I imagine him telling me something about how long he's carried a notebook in his pocket, or something else factual, something trivial even: like his best birthday ever or the day of the week he likes least. I stop and look at his newspaper. His finger has something trapped on the page. The name of one place, among the vast frontier of all the others. I just stare at it. This is the moment we're in: the improbable puzzle we're trying to crack.

"The police couldn't figure out the dentist the first time," I say quietly. It's nearly a whisper. "It took them a year to find his—"

He's gone, either way. Nothing will bring him back.

"I'm really sorry about your message. *Really.*" I hear the paper crash. "Claire, what's wrong?"

My mouth feels so dry. I shake my head.

"Oh," he says. "You don't—want to know any more about that night?"

I don't look at his face. I look at his hands. His skin is cracked and peeling. Is that something that happens to all rowers? And what does it mean that he's been biting his nails? There's just so much you can know about someone from looking at his hands.

"Let's check it out." He flips open his laptop. "Here, come sit next to me." He motions with his hand to the couch next to him. I watch his hand do this, call me over.

I feel my legs start to move, my heels touching down. I do all I can to stop them. I don't want to feel myself sitting next to him.

"I can see from here," I say. I feel myself exhale. My shoulders feel heavier as I shift on my seat across from him so that I see the screen at an angle. He looks at me, but I look at the letters of the Innernet's logo, which are spindly and New Age. They seem to imply serenity.

"Caffeine and inner peace. That's so Providence," I say, trying to make my voice cheerful. It just comes out strange.

I feel him looking at me, not the screen. I expect him to say something any second now.

It's so gray, I want to say in my real, right-now voice. *I need another vacation, Tate. Can we tutor or something?* But I don't. I can't even think of how to make a joke. I swallow. I look at his finger, the way it points to a single word in a sea of words. That's what it's like thinking about Richy. *I want to leave all this grayness, you know, Tate?* I want to move on.

"Listen, I really do have to get going. But thanks for this. I'll check out their website. I'll let you know if I spot something."

I pick up my bag and pull all of my layers back securely around my body. Maybe it *is* possible to lose something you never had.

"Claire, are you sure you're okay?" He seems genuinely stumped.

I shrug. "Exams. I'm tired of taking high school tests," I say. "I'll be okay as soon as I can get away." I look up for a brief second. "You know, out of high school."

When I leave, I notice the sun has quit trying to break through the clouds. The wet sidewalk is strewn with earthworms that had been washed out of the mud and marooned by the rain. Looking at the worms, I remember those cues from nature my father was talking about. I only see a downside to following impulses brought on by nature. I see that following cues gets you hurt.

"I decided I'll tell my father and let him take it from there. He'll know how to get it cleaned and everything. He'll kill me, but he'll help me first. I have to start straightening things out one at a time, or nothing will ever get straight."

Tess is in training, so she's doing a thousand sit-ups.

"I just wanted to say goodbye," I say, "just in case."

She stops in the middle of pulling up from the ground. In an amazing, effortless way, she holds her body folded in half, defying all rules of gravity. "Stop it. You're scaring me. Why now?"

"Tate," I say. "He's trying to have a life and this is getting in the way. I want to make sure he's not connected to any of this. I can make sure there's no trail back to him—or that's what I'm hoping for."

"Why not wait till the school year is over, till you graduate? Be safe."

"That's what I was thinking at first, but it's better to do it now—before anything else happens. A clean break."

"Then you'll explain it to your father, and he'll find a way to help you."

"I don't know how to start explaining." I look at her. She's still suspended mid-sit-up, her elbows sticking out of the sides of her head. "He'll probably send me off to a hospital for counseling. He'll have to make it some kind of posttraumatic thing." I shrug. "It could keep me out of jail."

She stops. Sits up. I see one of her hands come up to her mouth. "You won't be going—to college?"

I feel the weight of that in my chest. "It could possibly only be a slight interruption. Maybe just the summer in therapy. I'll get a lot of reading done. I'll learn watercolor technique. It won't be terrible. The only thing is, that story will stay with me forever—*how I was damaged.*"

"No," she says. "You're not *damaged.* You're Claire."

"I *am* Claire. One hundred percent." I look at her very sad face. And then I see *Tate's* face, the new one, with evidence of sunburn. The way his eyes are like water—how they change with the weather. I know I have to stop seeing them.

Giving back the dress will help with that.

"You know, I'm not even worried about that part. I'm thinking about how I can do this as fast as possible. I've decided—I need to do this quickly, before I chicken out."

She scrambles to her feet. "You're sure?"

"Yes. My father needs to know. He'll help—at least, I think he will. And I'm not exactly sure how much, but there's a piece of this that belongs to him, too."

"I meant about Tate. You're sure about *him*—wanting to get on with things. Shouldn't you talk to him?"

I find myself laughing for some reason. "We've talked a lot. I'm pretty sure I need to do this more than I need to talk."

"But you won't see him anymore after there's no dress."

"That's right," I say. "That's reality."

Chapter 20

THE JONES LIBRARY IS WARM and dry compared with the rest of the world, which has been preparing to dissolve after so many days of rain. The paper in the printer trays clumps together and makes the old people fussy.

I log on to the computer and start typing a paper on William Carlos Williams. I don't type *His mother had a sense of humor about his name*. I do type *a red wheel barrow glazed with rain water*. I'm not sure why I'm bothering. I'm probably not finishing the year . . . The overhead lights buzz. It's a dangerous, electric sound. I imagine my father's voice:

Why did you steal the dress, Claire?

I blink hard, and I type *I'm sorry I ate the plums*.

Because of sadness, is what I could say. An ocean of it.

I look up. I'd like to look out a window. This room has no windows but a skylight, with just those heavy clouds overhead, a disappointing kind of view.

I could not even see land. Do you understand that? How I could not see land?

I change to a new screen. A search. I type in *Innernet* and *Providence*.

I see the Zen of the Innernet logo. I see a drawing of steam rising from the outline of a powder-blue cup. An outline of hands embraces that cup. What it says is that the hands will feel the warmth. It's a good place.

I have this dress because you feel the power of that ocean, and after a while that ocean pulls you in.

I click on the video box. I lean very close to the screen, looking all over the Innernet. But it's a dark room.

Ask my mother about that pull.

Maybe I will see Richy in the audience. I want to. So much.

Oh. You can't.

Someone is talking on that video: Dennis, the manager, has introduced himself. He is welcoming us into that dark room and standing under a yellow light. It's open mic night at the coffee-house tonight.

I cross my arms over my chest. I pull them tight.

To-ni-eet.

Something about the sound of the word makes me laugh. I click on the arrow so the video starts again. Because I think I'm making a big mistake.

Because I think it's all a mistake. This is what I say to myself: *It's so dark, really, and it's all about the sound.* Who knows about the sound?

To-ni-eet.

Part of my chest deflates.

To-ni-eet, performing at the Innernet . . .

Why?

I don't think my heart is beating anymore. There is the sound of chatter, animals, squirrels, small birds. Something's grinding. Is this in my head?

I rewind.

My breathing has stopped and I am walking away from the video playing. The sound of it gets far away quickly. It feels good to be leaving, but it's tough to move through the room. Like walking through waves.

I am trying to get to the desk, where Patricia, my supervisor, is busy.

"Air—" I manage to say.

She barely looks up. "Take a break."

Outside it's dark and a fine mist filters the streetlight that's flickering in the bad light. Night and day have blended into a confusing mess. I try to suck some of the thick air into my throat. Any air. I tumble onto the slick bench. I bend over, crushing my nose into my knees. It's good to feel the pain of this for some reason. The pain feels normal. But that's all that's normal. I smash my nose in harder. I lift up my head and push it all the way back on my neck, try to force my lungs to work. I feel the cool mist on my face. I bend over again, pushing air out by pressing my chest with my arms. I hear my breathing—waves crashing. That's what's inside my head. Crashing. It's so hot on this cold street. When I lift my head again I see Tate's face, upside down.

"Claire." He's sitting on the bench, I think. He's talking even though I'm like this. His seeing is impaired? He's saying—he's saying *the bench is wet*—he just noticed—*it was about my sister,* he's saying—and he might be shaking me. He's saying other things, I think, but I'm confused. So confused. I feel his hands on my arms. He's trying to wake me out of this. But the shaking is making the crashing worse.

"Claire, what's happening to you?"

I fill my lungs with air. Too much air. I try hard to exhale.

"It's not dentist," I force out. "It's *Dennis.*"

Chapter 21

"I can't go back," I say. Now I seem to be shaking him. I have the front of his jacket in my hands while I'm shaking him.

"It's okay. Wait a minute. Catch your breath."

I stop shaking him, but I don't let go of his shirt. I mustn't.

"What happened to you? Did something happen with the dress?"

Now I feel my heart beating. Hard.

"No," I say. "I wish."

"Then what?"

"That video. From that place. I watched it. Just now."

"You saw him? He was there?"

I feel myself nodding slowly, looking over his shoulder at the spotlights that shine on the Jones Library sign. It's day and night at the same time, because of the rain and the clouds.

"We should let the police know that Richy was there—"

"No. NO." I squeeze my eyes shut. "*Not Richy.* I was hoping to see Richy, but—"

"Claire, what are you talking about? You're not making sense."

"I saw him. The guy he was going to meet."

His hands come up to mine, where I'm clutching his shirt. I feel them cover up my hands. I won't let go. He can't make me. "Claire, you—you never saw that guy. What are you talking about?"

I feel the weight of my heart in my chest. "I heard him. I heard his voice. That's the guy he was meeting. I heard the message, Tate." My voice is ragged.

I feel my hands between his. I take a breath and let his shirt go.

His head is tilted, and the mist has matted his hair close to his scalp and made it darker, so that he looks like someone I don't know in this confusing light. Someone who's holding on to my hands.

"You believe me, don't you? Just say you believe me."

"Yes," he says. "I do. Let's go in and get your things."

"She's sick," Tate says when we go back inside the library.

Patricia's eyes get so round.

"I found her on the sidewalk," he says.

"On the *sidewalk*?" Her whisper is urgent.

"On a bench outside," he corrects.

One of his arms is wrapped around my waist, the other clutches my laptop. I am floppy. This is an uncommon sight for the patrons of the Jones Library. I look at the floor when I realize their faces reveal their terror.

"I'll take her home."

Patricia makes her head crooked to match up to my crooked head. *"Do you know this man?"* Her whisper is imperative.

"He's my . . . friend," I say.

She wrinkles her nose at him. It's a librarian's snarl.

"Make sure she gets home *safely*," she whispers, but he's already dragging me out the door.

"He's the dentist?" Tate asks. We are at my house.

I cannot speak as I watch the video. *Welcome to this week's Innernet Café Open Mic. To-ni-eet* . . .

I watch it again.

"His name is Dennis," I say. "He says it here." I point at the screen. "You found it. How could the police not? How could he look like everybody else?" He does. He has brown hair the color of mouse fur and a small nose that comes to a tiny peak in the middle of his face. He looks like one sample of something mass-produced: he looks like everyone.

I watch it again. *To-ni-eet.* It's a sound that carries right through all of my cells, sets them sideways, wrong.

"You have the voice part," he says. "Nobody has that but you."

I look at him, his face. "You believe me? You don't think I'm wishing this is true. That I want it so badly I'm imagining it?"

"Of course I don't. Let's call the police. Or better yet, we'll go to the police in Providence. I'll drive."

"NO." I feel my hands coming up to my cheeks. "The police will think I'm crazy. I don't want—it all to happen again."

I look at the screen.

Is this the last person to see Richy? Is it?

I cover my eyes with my hands. I won't move them. If I can see, the past will flood back.

Providence, where the strange fog stayed close to the ground, in a story from up a beanstalk, the bare trees, hairy where they met the sky, the cars gliding on cloud tops. A grim fairy tale.

What do you know about Richy, Claire?

Fee, fie, foe, fum.

You were the last one to see him.

Richy's father coming for me. I'll huff and I'll puff and I'll blow the door down.

"Claire?"

I squeeze my eyes shut.

Claire, Claire, you're barely there.

Could I stop her somehow?

Could I put it off just another day? . . . *Have her for one more day?*

Could I say, *Richy, don't go. It's cold. Don't go. If I say that, if I say please, please don't . . .*

"Claire?"

I feel cold, so cold, like I am lying on stone on a winter day.

"Claire."

I rub my face as if it were clay. I remodel it, make it into somebody else's. Then something warm surrounds me, like I'm under warm water but I can still breathe. I smell green—peppermint and grass.

Tate's big arms spread wide around me, my whole head tucked inside them, and melting.

After a long time, I feel the hold loosening.

"A car . . ." His voice is low and rough.

Oh.

The living room and Tate are soft and liquid, a blurred picture.

Outside, I hear laughing, two birds. One bigger. His hand lingers on my back for one last moment, then he gets up. I hear keys in the lock and the front door opens.

"Oh," my dad says when he sees Tate. He still has his Grace smile in his eyes, though. He's almost disguising his surprise at finding us here together.

"We picked up sushi," Grace says. She shakes off her raincoat, and underneath she's wearing flowing clothes, as usual. She's carrying a large brown bag. She flows over to the couch where I sit, and Tate stands. "Have you had dinner yet?"

My dad doesn't stop looking at me. He thinks my body and soul have been through something. I can see this in his eyes.

He knows me.

"Should we get some dishes?" Grace says. I hear the crinkle of the bag. But no one moves. She looks at my father, and then at me, and then at Tate. I hear her voice get just a little louder. "Mark, help me find the wasabi?" As he follows her into the kitchen, I still smell mint.

"So you were presenting again?" I hear Tate raising his voice so that Grace can hear in the next room. In this room he shakes his head at me, trying to tell me something.

I hear Grace from the kitchen, and my father speaking over her.

"It was just a small thing," she says.

"You're crazy. I could barely get you out of that room, so many people wanted to speak to you." He's back to her. Good.

Tate motions with his hand. I see him look into the dining room and then move over to the couch, where I sit.

I am watching him, but also imagining being near Richy's killer, his brown mouse hair, the way he looks like anyone in a store, on a train. I shiver.

I feel Tate shift on the sofa cushion as he leans close to me. "The laptop," he says. I watch his hand in front of me, lowering the screen, which still has the Innernet logo. "What lie will you be telling your father?" Tate whispers. "Not the one about why I'm here. The one after that."

I hear the music start.

"I know you're going there." He leans closer to me and whispers. "No one is going to stop you. You *aren't* going without me." His eyes lock me in.

"Anybody out there want some green tea?" Grace's voice travels from the kitchen.

"Okay," I whisper. "I won't go—without you."

"Okay, then, Saturday?" I feel his hand grip my arm. "Promise me you'll wait until Saturday."

"So you didn't tell your dad—about the dress—yet?" Tess asks.

"No—something came up. It's—that Richy thing. I need to go check something out. Tate's willing to drive. I told my dad I need to go shopping, to get some clothes. That always works."

Tess is leaning way back in her chair, the look of vague amusement on her face. "*Willing* . . . right . . ."

"I'll fill you in when we get back—"

"Just don't elope," she says, leaning forward with her head balanced on one hand, but she's not looking at me. She's looking through me. "Stay where you are, *on the verge.* Stay there as long as you can."

"Uh—there's no *verge*," I mumble, but she's not listening. She's somewhere else now. "What is it, Tess—Gus?"

"Oh," she says, "it's just college." She bats at the air. But she knows her words have a kind of artificial sweetness to them, so she looks down, and then up. "I didn't know him when I sent out applications."

"And?"

She looks at me. "He'll be in California . . . And I'll be at Vassar. It's so far . . ."

"You'll take it as it comes along," I say. "That's all. You'll take care of it one thing at a time. And you have the whole summer first."

"You're right," she says, but her whole face isn't smiling. "Anyway, just tell your dad you and I are going to Boston. Tell him there's a *huge* J. Crew outlet there. He ought to like that."

Chapter 22

IT'S ONE OF THOSE FRAGILE spring days, where the light is weak and hazy. The air is cold, but not the deep kind of cold, and the woods are still bare.

"Stop thinking about what happens when we get there. You don't know what will happen, so stop imagining." Tate's in the driver's seat.

"I never stop imagining." My stomach burns. "It's part of my curse."

"So how is the writing going?" he asks.

"What makes you think I'm writing at all?" I cross my arms and look out the window.

"Claire." He laughs. "I know you pretty well now . . ."

My stomach burns more. I feel myself sinking deeper into my jacket.

"I miss reading your writing. I'll have to buy your books someday. I'll see one in a bookstore and I'll say, 'I knew her.'"

I knew her. I hear myself sigh.

"When you're famous and you don't remember—"

"I won't be—" I start to say.

"Sure you'll be famous. I'll bet on it. When you are, you won't remember all the little people . . ."

Able to forget you, is what I'm thinking, *even if I wanted to.* I close my eyes and lean against the car window. The weak sunlight blinks through the bare trees. I can feel it on my closed eyelids. "You're not," I say, quietly, *"so little."*

He laughs. "I'm serious. About your writing. I saw myself in it, even though it was your life."

"Saw yourself?" I look over at him. "How could *anyone* see—"

He's looking at the road, but somewhere else, too.

His hands shift on the steering wheel, his fingers regripping.

"I'm tired—" I start. I hear the snag in my voice. My throat is telling me to stop. "I'm tired of always being—in that room with that mirror." I bite into my lip. I really should stop talking. "All I can see is me, and you—" I look down. I can't possibly look at him. "You have the two-way view. It's a better deal for you, I think."

"It's like that for people in a fan club," he says. It's a joke, I know, but the way he says it makes it sound like something else. Like there's a real club and it's a life-or-death thing.

"Do you think it's fair?"

He's leaning way back in his seat with his arms stretched out in front of him, straight. "I think *you* don't," he says.

"I think—" I feel my heart beating faster. "That you're in another club, too."

He sits up straight. It's a very slight movement. That's his only response.

I go on. "On the day you met me at Emily Dickinson's grave, do you remember? In September. You asked this: 'What's the measure of your grief?' I think it was only *kind of* a joke."

The weak sunlight colors his profile and the whole car with pink-yellow, in quick flashes.

"That club," I say.

He lets one long breath escape from between his lips.

"You know what I mean," I say. "I know you do—you know too much about the club."

"You are—" he starts. "You're a little like someone I used to know . . ."

"Who?"

He presses his lips together tightly. "She's gone."

"Oh—I'm sorry. You don't have to." I shake my head. "Is that why you asked all those questions—at the beginning?"

"Your writing," he says, "brought it all back. I've been trying to leave all that behind me."

"That's why." I feel the power of this in my chest. It feels over-sized for that place. "*That's* why you followed me."

He shrugs.

When he was looking at me, it was another person he was seeing.

It's like the camera moves back, and I see the set. I understand just where we are in this movie. It's a place I had imagined—*or wished?*—was different. I think I see that place clearly, until I hear him say this: "That's why, *at first*. But then you broke my nose."

"I did?" Now the movie set is changing again. It's big—and whatever new things are happening, they're blurry.

"Yeah—you remember. Cows? Vermont? Blood?"

I feel my eyes blinking, trying to see clearly.

"That's when I knew," he says.

I turn my head down toward the floor, without looking at him, hoping he doesn't see my face, how unraveled he's made it. *I knew something after that, too. You tell me what you knew, first.* I close my eyes.

The car takes on the sound of wailing as we shift onto a metal bridge and then the tension of the tires on the metal sounds like whistling.

"Well, here we go," I hear him say.

I open my eyes. A big sign welcomes us to Providence.

"Are you ready?" he asks.

Chapter 23

PING-PONG BALLS BOUNCE OFF all of my organs as I sit in the window of the Innernet Café. It is a dark place with lots of different colors of wood, and even the scent of sandalwood curling around the coffee brewing and bread toasting. Under other circumstances, with a cup of herbal tea, you could get some inner peace in this place.

But not today.

"What if he's not working today? What if he doesn't work here anymore? What if he moved? What if—"

"Claire, it's okay any way it goes. We came for information. We're trying to find out what happened that night. That's all. I'll start talking to the people behind the counter. I'll tell them I'm a reporter writing about open mic nights in the area—tell them I saw the video and the ad in the paper."

After Tate leaves, I look out the window, Ping-Pong balls still jumping. I see an early spring day on a street full of ordinary things: stiff shirts covered in dry-cleaning bags walk by, and optimistic sunglasses with two pictures of the sky. It *is* spring, I keep reminding myself—my last-last year of high school is all but over.

But here I am, stuck in the past, snagged by the holes in my life—these places where the people were cut out. Why can't I stop getting stuck on these missing pieces?

I look at the table in front of me. My soda is sweating a big puddle on the dark tabletop and the sky is reflected there, too, or at least a patch of it. It's like a Post-it note reminding me: the sun comes back, eventually, whether you believe it or not. It has for my father, anyway.

I look over at the counter, where Tate's standing, laughing at the right parts, asking relevant questions. The guy there seems happy to answer them.

Is there someone here named Dennis?

Do I want there to be?

What if he left months ago?

Do I wish that's true?

I shut my eyes tightly. When I open them again, I am looking at the floor. An unsuspecting foot is about to step on my backpack, which has dropped off the back of the chair. I move my hand to snatch it back. I see the wood slats, my backpack, and something else. I blink.

I blink again.

HHHHH.

I breathe in so deeply I'm sure everyone in the place hears. It comes with a sharp stinging feeling.

My hand is one foot away from Richy's shoes.

I think the shoes pause as I make the noise, but then they continue—*ca-lick, ca-lick*.

I watch as the shoes walk away from me. For a moment, they are gone—are they something I have imagined? All I see is two legs of jeans, and the jeans cover the backs of the shoes. *Ca-lick, ca-lick*. Then the feet turn.

I am at this point still leaning over toward the ground, and all the blood in my body is pooled and pulsing.

Is Richy alive? Was it all a mistake?

I shoot up, seated, my body turned at the waist. My eyes must be so wide.

Richy's shoes are there, yes, but not on Richy, on someone else, someone who looks familiar.

Oh. NO. Thin brown hair, like mouse fur.

I see his profile as he talks to the people behind the counter. I cannot hear his voice, but I know it's Dennis.

Tate is there, too, but facing in the other direction, talking to one of the staff.

The shoes pivot. He spins on their fancy heels. He puts one hand in the pocket of his jeans. The other one sways as he walks down the corridor to the back of the building. My Ping-Pong balls activate. They are almost audible when Tate comes back to the table.

"You're very—*pink*," he says. He wiggles his fingers around his cheeks to show me where.

I can feel my mouth is open. I make it a point to close my mouth. To swallow. To breathe.

He looks at me, eyebrows crunched, head tilted. "What?"

"He's *here*," I whisper. I motion with my head to the hallway to the left of the counter. "He just came through the front door. He's gone back there."

Tate looks up, but the corridor leads to shadows.

"Well, this is very good," Tate says, leaning back in his chair. He loops his elbows over the back. "We know where he is, Claire." He nods decisively. "We don't have to go looking for him."

I lean forward so low my chin is nearly in the puddle from my soda.

"Claire," he says. His voice is hushed. "It's all right. He can't hurt you. Calm down. Your eyes are scary. They're very big and very—"

"Richy didn't kill himself. Finally I'm going to prove it." I say this with all the air I have left in my lungs and then I take a deep, quick breath. "That guy—he's wearing *Richy's shoes*."

Chapter 24

"THAT'S HIM." I LOOK at Tate instead of Dennis. Tate looks down. He's confused.

"You're sure?"

I look at Dennis. "Yes, don't you recognize him from the video?"

"Yeah—he's got less hair now," he says. "But, Claire, he's wearing sneakers. I think they're Nikes."

"You don't think I'm crazy, do you? You believe me, don't you—you believe I saw Richy's shoes? They are tan, Italian, very fancy—" I am clutching the edge of the table so hard that I might snap it off. "What if I am seeing things—making things make sense, *forcing sense* into things?"

He reaches across the table. He puts his hands over my white knuckles and squeezes. It's a gesture that could go either way, I think, until he says this:

"You go talk to him. Ask him about working here or something. He must have changed in the back. I'm going to find Richy's shoes."

Ah.

He's going to find Richy's shoes.

In the middle of all this, my heart blossoms. It's one of those irreversible moments, I know—the moment my little canoe just starts to tip over the waterfall. For me, there won't be any turning back.

I watch as Tate calmly stands and walks over to the counter. He's all Neo from *The Matrix*. He says, "Restrooms this way?" and motions with his head down the corridor.

I get to my feet. I have been sweating so much that all of my clothing is glued to me. I'm numb and hot and feel like wood. You could slice my fingers off and I wouldn't know it. I make an attempt to fluff myself up, pulling my clothes away from my skin with my fingertips. Across the room, Dennis's head is ducking inside a cabinet.

Now I feel a chill, like a wave, run over all my skin starting from my wrists and working up to my scalp and down to my knees.

I walk over to the cabinet, where one of his arms is holding on to the handle. It's all I can see of him: his one hairy forearm—hair, light and abundant, like ash. This detail makes me need to vomit.

"Are you the manager?" My voice is shaking and small. He looks around the cabinet door. I see his eyes. They are like small pellets. They are bored with me.

He says, "Yes."

The familiar sound of his voice stuns me. On the Internet, it seemed cosmic and dangerous. But here the voice that gives routine information—about restoring your seats to their upright position, or flossing after meals—repeating the information so often I know the script by heart.

This whole scene, in fact, is playing exactly as it was written. It feels fated that I am so near to Richy's killer I could break his nose. That all the hairs on my body are rising.

"Any openings?" I ask. My voice squeaks. "I'm looking for a job."

His eyes leave my face and start to travel down to my toes. I close my eyes.

When I open them, he is looking back in the cabinet, the door a barrier between us.

"No," he says into the cabinet. Over Dennis's shoulder I see Tate coming out of the shadows in the corridor toward the table. I turn and follow him. He hands me my backpack from the floor and takes my hand. He leads me out into the dull sun of the street in front of the Innernet.

The scene on the street is louder than I'd like it to be. Confusing and pastel and faded.

"Walk quickly," he says, pulling me down the street.

"What? Wait—"

"Come on." He tugs on my elbow. "Richy's feet were a couple of sizes smaller than mine."

I look down at the blurred tangle of Tate's and my moving feet.

"It was the easiest way to get them out," he says.

Now *he's* wearing Richy's shoes.

When I come out of the drugstore with replacement shoes because Tate left his behind, he's got Richy's shoes on the dashboard. He's staring at them.

"Trophies . . ." he says as I get into my seat. Now we are both staring at the Italian loafers, the color of café au lait in the sun. "Some killers do that. Collect things. But it's evidence, right? I mean, if these were Richy's."

I think back to the day we met at Emily Dickinson's grave. People make rubbings from her gravestone. "They are—were. I'm sure." I look at the shoes. "As creepy as it is, the way we got them, I'm happy to have a piece of Richy here with us."

Once these words leave my mouth, I brace myself for the impact of how weird that must have sounded. *Who says something like that?* I try to stuff myself between the seats, like coins.

But then I stop. I sit up. I think for a minute.

Who says something like that?

I do. *I* say something like that.

This is who I am—not *this is what life has made me*, but who I am.

Me.

I take one of the shoes in my hand and touch it to my cheek. I press it against my skin.

Richy was on his way to my house. As I looked out the door, I could see his feet lifting off the pedals as he came down the street like a great big skinny bird on that bike, all wings and angles. His hair was blowing all around. His eyebrows high, his mouth in an O.

It was October seventh, see? The anniversary. So I was making a movie in my head. And he knew that.

And he knew I was having trouble speaking.

He had Orangina in his bag and clear plastic cups. He had Goldfish crackers and cookies in the shape of seashells. "Eat with elegance," he instructed me. So we sat up tall on the blanket he had spread on the ground. We sipped our fizzy drinks. The trees around us were just starting to turn, the bottom leaves still green.

"Watch those trees," he said, pointing. "If you sit very quietly they'll do a magic act. They'll change color for you."

We sat very still, not talking.

It happened a little at a time, over the course of an hour. Nobody said a word.

By six o'clock the trees were completely the color of the sun.

Glowing—

Yellow *wouldn't be a good enough word.*

He leaned over, close to me, without touching—he understood about that.

He said, "See? It's not the worst day of the year."

The caramel leather on the shoe I am holding has dark spots all of a sudden. I rub my eyes.

"Richy's mom will know they're his," I say, nodding. My voice is rusty and old. "It's not far to their house." I look over at Tate.

He's looking at me and the shoe. His cheeks are wet.

Chapter 25

WE ARE PARKED ON THE STREET outside Richy's house—the house where Richy lived.

"What if his dad is home? What if he tries to strangle you?" Tate asks.

"It's not that way. He thought I had something to do with his son disappearing," I say. "My dad would probably do the same thing. Wouldn't yours?"

"Eh, no," he mumbles.

"What?"

"Nothing. Uh, should we go knock? I hope the right person is home."

"Um, Tate, just one thing—" The dogs next door are growling, getting ready to greet us. I can hear their chains snaking along the fence. "I'm going to call you Sam. Okay?"

I hear him chuckling. "Yeah."

* * *

When Richy's mom opens the door I see her face reflect a year in time-lapse photography. First she's flat, like a dish, like the world is something animated and she's the object, with eyes surrounded by shadows. But then she figures out it's me, the one who came for spaghetti and the one whose chin she touched, gently. The one she doubted. The one she suspected. But, then, she was missing a boy, you see? And—not that it matters—*her only boy*.

"I sent you an e-mail about the memorial," she says quickly. Her eyes at this point are large black buttons.

"I got it," I say. "Thank you. I came. We came—" I move my fingers in the air back and forth between me and Tate. "But we stayed outside. My father didn't—"

Now her face drops. "I know. You were afraid," she says. "I'm ashamed of that. But Richy's dad doesn't live here anymore." When she looks back up, it's a desperate look, like something in the world is still worth that kind of effort, like some part of her broken heart still pumps. "But you're here now." Do I even see her smile?

"I'm not—" I reach out to her arm. I feel my hand there, on the sleeve of her blouse. "I'm not afraid."

Out of the corner of my eye I can see Tate is watching my face. "I know this isn't going to make much sense, but I have these shoes . . ." I pull the loafers out of my backpack. "Mrs. DiMarco, I think they're Richy's."

Tate and I are sitting on the bed, surrounded by what Richy left behind. Everything is the same as the last time I was here except for the drawings of the big boots. The folding table is empty. You'd never know about the zippers.

His mother is frantically lifting the lids off shoe boxes. "Richy kept his shoes in their original boxes," I tell Tate. "It was important to him. I know he was wearing them that night," I say louder. The Italian loafers are on my lap. "I can see him. He wore green socks with orange diamonds. He drove the ducks crazy."

Tate's head gets tilty.

"Long story," I say.

"They aren't here anywhere," she says, her voice hollow in the closet. Her face is sunken in at the seams. The circles under her eyes look like tattoos. She flops on the bed between where Tate and I sit. She lies all the way back, her knees bent, her legs dangling from the edge of the bed.

"I'm sorry to be dragging all this—"

"*Wait.*" She shoots upright like a drawbridge gone haywire, and disappears out of the room.

In a second she's back with a photograph. Richy at Christmas with the shoes. "There's a small rip near the toe. That's why he could afford them. Factory seconds from the outlet. You can see it. Right here."

"There, on the left foot," Tate says.

"Just a minute," she says. "Where did you get these?"

The dogs next door erupt. I feel a wave of chills. I look into her cloudy eyes. "I know who killed him. We got the shoes from his office."

"WHAT? WHO?"

"We stole them—" Tate interrupts.

"You think you know—" Richy's mom is saying. "I don't under-stand—"

"They were never *his*," I say to Tate. I turn to Richy's mom.

"His name is Dennis. I heard his voice, on Richy's phone. It's a long story, but we put the pieces together."

"We're going to the police right now," Tate says, standing.

"But how—and this guy, this Dennis. Why would the police believe he had the shoes if you've got them?" she asks.

"Oh," Tate says, deflating. He sits back on the bed as I jump to my feet.

"We've got to get them back there. Right away."

"Wait," Richy's mom says quickly. Her voice is high and crazy. "I'm coming, too."

The afternoon crowd is small at the Innernet, about half full of people typing away on laptops, here for a little caffeine to go with their inner peace. Richy's mom and I take a seat while Tate goes to the counter and gets the drinks, checking out where Dennis is.

I'm shaking.

"What if he went out for lunch," I say, "and noticed the missing shoes?"

Richy's mom has her button eyes—big and round and lined with shadows. She sits on the edge of her chair. She presses the palms of her hands flat on the cold tabletop. She seems to be holding it down.

Tate brings three tall drinks with ice to the table.

"Hey, you," we hear. My heart stops still. We all look up at the counter. Tate turns as if in slow motion. I am ready for the gunshots to ring out, but instead the guy behind the counter says, "Your straws."

Tate forgot the prop straws for the prop drinks at the counter. He goes back.

When he returns to the table, he looks at me, holds my look for a minute while his hand moves to the backpack. He slides it over his shoulder and turns. He walks toward the corridor.

I stop breathing.

Coming out of the shadow of the same hallway is Dennis. I watch as they bump shoulders. I see this in slow motion, I swear. Tate keeps walking. Dennis, though, stops. I watch him look at the ceiling for a second, then I watch as his sneakers pivot and he turns back. To the dark hallway.

To where Tate is heading.

"No."

"That's him, isn't it?" Richy's mom has the voice of empty rooms, full of a deep empty echo. Her hand clutches at my arm tightly. She moves her other hand to my shoulder and then she's got both my shoulders. She's shaking me.

"THAT'S HIM."

The man at the table next to us hisses at his computer screen. I watch him jump out of his seat. In a different tragedy, he's spilled his coffee on his laptop.

"*That's him*," Richy's mom is hissing. Her nostrils are flared, her ears bright red.

At the same time I hear something like boxes falling, I see Tate running to the front of the store, the zipper of the backpack flapping open, Dennis in pursuit. Dennis grabs the back of Tate's shirt and Tate spins backwards. Tate steps back, back. Dennis is shouting, pinning Tate to the front door of the store. He's shorter than

Tate, but leaning into him like a mean attack dog, leading with his mouse head, his teeth bared.

"What were you doing in there?" he's shouting. "You were there this morning. What the hell were you doing in my office?"

The customers have cleared the front-door area.

"You and that girl." He points toward me. "I saw you leave together." He pulls Tate's shirt and Tate steps backwards, off balance.

What do you do when you see, for yourself, the reason you have lost the person you loved most?

You reach for whatever you can get your hands on.

Richy's mom is standing, her head not moving, her eyes trained on the back of Dennis's head. But her arm is moving, her hand reaching for the back of a chair. She lifts the weightless chair and turns slightly. This part seems to be happening in slow motion—the way the chair loops in a circle before it takes flight.

Then a split second of nothing—not even breathing. That moment I brace for impact is utterly silent. But then the iron chair shatters the plate-glass window in layers of shrieks, like awful music. The chair keeps going, veers into the car parked in front. A second impact, the clash of metal on metal, and glass again. And then after a pause, when everything settles, the sparkling sound of a cascade of glass shards in the aftershock.

Sirens, then, start like rumors and collect in the margins, working their way to the very loud center of it all. Another set of sirens.

Sirens, again.

Police are here, weeding through people, with angry faces. Before one of them gets a grip on him, Tate whispers in my ear.

Richy's shoes are in the office. He doesn't know a thing.

I pull on Richy's mom's arm. "Don't say anything about the shoes. It'll be okay." I stare into her stunned eyes. They are full of police lights. Her face seems stopped, emptied of all expression except relief.

Something that held her has let her go.

But she still does not know how to be free of her captor. She looks around the room for answers.

I find her eyes. I grasp her arm tightly.

"Nothing about the shoes," she repeats, to let me know she gets it.

My dad looks helpless, like tiny ropes are pulling down the corners of his eyes and cheeks and lips.

"What time is it?" I ask. "This day has lasted a hundred and forty years." I lean my head on Tess's shoulder and she puts her arm around me. We are sitting on a bench in the storeroom of the coffee shop. They have summoned my father from Amherst, and he has come to Providence, this time with reinforcements.

It seems like years instead of hours since it all happened . . .

When I open my eyes I see Grace, flowing into the room, which is filled with cardboard boxes and sacks of coffee beans. She wears shoes with ribbons that tie around her ankles. I'm so tired, all I can do is stare at those ribbons and watch her feet lightly cover the pattern on the floor tiles. Every other tile is tan. Her feet stop in front of me.

I am surrounded by them: my dad on my right, Tess on my left, and Grace in front of me.

"They found Richy's bag—so many of his things . . . He didn't even bother to hide it." My dad looks at me, still sagging. It seems his face might drip right off his bones.

"Do you want a bagel?" Grace asks me. I hear paper crumpling. "Or some tea?"

I feel itchy all over my body, my arms, my legs, the bottoms of my feet.

"Are there people still out there? Did the police take—anyone—away?"

"Claire," my dad says. "He's not here anymore."

"Are you sure?"

"He's in jail," my dad says. "But you should know—this thing is very big—"

"Who? Who's in jail?" I hear my voice, the urgency in it.

"Claire, this story—"

"Tate? Did they take Tate to jail? They separated us. I haven't seem him since— Tess, have you seen him? Can you go look around for Tate?"

I look at Tess. Her eyes are charged.

"Claire, you have to be ready." I hear my father's voice get louder, insisting upon attention, but I look at Tess. She's shaking her head. I hear my father's voice as I watch her face.

"Word has spread very quickly," my dad says, more steadily now. "It's a big story." I watch Tess's eyes watch him.

"You should know that you are at the center of it," he says. "They want you to get ready to go to the police station. You have to be prepared when you get there."

"What?" I'm looking at Tess's face for these answers. She's still looking at my dad.

"Claire." My dad touches my hands. "As you can imagine, there's interest in the story in Providence, it's one of those stories that get attention . . ."

"Just—if I could see Tate. See if he's—"

"I haven't seen him—but, Claire, I'm not sure you are understanding me. There are reporters already."

"What? Why?" I feel my head turning to Tess and then my dad and bouncing back again. I don't seem to be able to stop this.

"The murder case solved by the best friend—"

"No," I say. I close my eyes. I smell so much coffee. "This will be my story for life?"

Grace strokes my head.

"Why can't it just end?"

"I'm sorry, Claire," my father says, his hands gripping mine. I look at his eyes, draped by sagging skin.

I press my eyes shut tightly. I squeeze them.

"I can't," I say, "do this again." *Reliving it all, all the way back to the first time, the blood oranges, the creek . . .*

No.

But then Tess pulls away her arm and shakes me. She's waking me up. Her eyes are bright, electric and shining. She motions with her head to the right. "Here he comes."

It's Tate walking through the door. Even from across the storeroom I can see that little crease between his eyes disappear when he sees me. Or is this what I hope I see? It doesn't matter: Something about the way he looks—his gray T-shirt, his feet in those drugstore replacement shoes, his hair all crushed to his head—is so familiar, so *what I expect to see*, I have this feeling that I have known him all my life, maybe longer.

"This time, Claire," Tess says, "it's different. This time you have us."

* * *

The landmark for turning to the Providence police headquarters is the gray exterminator's building where a giant termite sits on the roof like an oracle. As much as it says we are back in Providence, it also reminds me how far away we are from last year.

Today the oracle tells me about how much things can change.

On the day we left Providence to go to Amherst, I had not left my house for four months. I remember how the rain came down in sheets as we drove away, how we could hardly see the yellow line in the middle of the road. How what we were leaving behind was as blurry as what was ahead.

But today it's spring, a different year, apparently a different lifetime. The sky I can see out Grace's van window is full of intermittent clouds that look like lace.

I am in the middle row of Grace's van, surrounded by boxes of old buttons and vintage tablecloths. Across the seat is Tess, her cheek resting on a pillow she's made of her sweatshirt. Grace is driving. My dad is pointing, talking, maybe remembering his old life here, making her a little bit more a part of his new life. Tate is in the back, waiting to take his part in the plan at the police station when we get there. Like everyone who meets up with an oracle, I am tempted to ask the giant termite for directions. Where am I headed next?

But I already have the answer: *You really don't want to know.*

The plan is that Tate and I will get out of the van one block ahead of the police station.

The strange part for me is how quiet it is on the street when we get out of Grace's big red van and watch it drive away. I understand that reporters are waiting for me a block away, but it feels improbable on this perfect spring day, the sun just about ready to set. I stand there, not knowing how to move forward. It's when he takes my arm and wraps it around his that I notice how I feel. I'm flexible, yes, but still wooden. I don't know how to do this part, so I try to make it funny. "You're a good disguise," I say. "Nobody in Providence will ever recognize me with somebody like—"

"You're shaking?" he says. His head tilts.

It's still warm air, so shivering doesn't make much sense.

"You're scared? I was sure nothing could scare you." He smiles, holds my arm tighter. I feel how strong he is.

I shake harder.

The police station is set back from the road and surrounded by a large parking lot. As we round the corner, I can see the van in the distance, driving slowly past the front steps of the police station. There seem to be a lot of people on the steps. "You've attracted quite a crowd," Tate says.

I squint.

"Grace wants to be sure they see the Massachusetts license plates."

Tate leans close to my ear, like he's telling me a secret, though a parking lot full of cars separates us from any other people. "Don't worry. They'll put on a good show in front and we'll slip through the back door without anyone seeing you. Come on."

I look at him. He looks ahead. He's very certain. He can see something off in the distance that I can't.

* * *

Tess is the decoy, posing as me.

Tate and I are walking toward the side of the station as we see them start up the steps. My dad has one arm, Grace the other, and Tess is in the middle, taller than either of them. Her curly black hair bounces as they make their way up the steps. Tess is smiling for the cameras. Because there are so many people to get through, the scene seems to be shot in slow motion.

I'm watching my life, recast as a shampoo ad with a beautiful girl, when I hear the shout come from the stairs. They have discovered their error.

I hear more shouting, and then Tate. "CLAIRE, RUN."

Tate's arm rounds my waist tightly. I feel us start to move fast. He's practically dragging me. It's just like that night in December, except I'm not wearing Emily Dickinson's dress, and this time somebody with a camera is chasing us, hoping we fall.

The narrow walkway we take to get to the back door has shrubs on one side. I close my eyes. I hear the sound of footsteps behind us.

Then I see the steps. I feel Tate twist me. He pushes my back against the corner. I hit the door so hard it sucks out all my breath. He turns his back to me. His whole body presses against mine, completely covering me.

I smell his shirt and feel the moisture of it. My cheek is against his spine. With him as a shield, it's very dark except around the edges, where the flashing cameras look like bombs in the night. Cameras are taking his picture while I hide behind him.

Inside the police station one gray room leads to another, like the series of events in a mundane dream. The window is a bright orange box holding the outside world at sunset. The two versions of the world, the slow gray inside and the vivid outside—like two lives—are parallel but separate, disconnected.

I am on one side of a long metal table and the bean-eyed police officer and his female partner are on the other.

"Wait," I say before we start. I look across the room where I can see what looks like a window to the gray hallway where my dad, Tate, Tess, and Grace are standing like a grove of trees. I know all they can see is themselves in the two-way mirror, but they aren't taking their eyes off the glass.

That's what faith looks like.

"Okay," I say. "Go ahead."

I hear the same sentence five times, five different men speaking from a room not far away. The fifth time the word lands, like a coin in a metal can. *To-ni-eet.* There's snag in the word. One of the letters pulled, like yarn in a sweater. Pulling at my heart. *Why would anyone hurt Richy?*

"That's him."

"You did something amazing," Beany Eyes tells me. His partner nods.

"I thought this would feel different. It won't bring him back," I say. "Now I see."

"No, it won't," the officer says. "But it's still something."

I walk around the corner, and it's nothing but gray walls and long hallways.

"Claire?" A voice from behind me. It's Richy's mother.

"I thought you'd gone. I didn't know if I would see you," I say.

"I was waiting for you. I wanted to say—" She looks remote,

like she's said goodbye to something far away, but she can't take her eyes off it.

"Can we sit?" she says, waving at a bench down one of the hallways.

"I wanted to say—"

She seems to be having trouble holding her head up. She's bent over. Looking at her hands. But then she manages to look up. *"Thank you,"* she says. "For not forgetting him."

"I never could," I say.

"He liked you so much," she said. She stops, takes a breath. "Do you think I'll ever get used to that?" she asks. "To talking about him in the past?"

I know what she means.

"Yes," I say. "You will." But I know that everybody leaves a different empty space. Some are big and heavy for a long time.

"Can I ask you something?"

"Okay," I say.

"There was so much I didn't know about him . . ." She looks down, her face full of shadows. "Can you tell me something I didn't know? Something I missed?"

I have grown a rock in my throat. It won't seem to move, no matter how hard I swallow. I take a deep breath and think. I look around at all this grayness.

Things come back in full, factual sentences:

Richy was wearing green socks with orange diamonds. Though Richy was an island, you needed to be gentle. Richy was never meant to be machine-washed. You had to be gentle. He was so gentle.

And then from far down the hallway, I see Tate. He walks toward us. I hold up my hand. He stops. He watches. I nod. I turn back to Richy's mom.

"There was this one night . . ." I start. I am thinking hard about what to say.

Her head tilts—*yes?*

"You made us spaghetti."

She nods. "Oh, yes, I remember."

"We had such a nice time."

"Yes."

I stop and think.

"And he walked me to my car," I say. "Which was parked under the streetlight outside that used to flicker—"

"Oh, it still does."

"It was flickering, I remember. It seemed like a movie effect. Every now and again our faces would be silver—" I stop.

"I can just picture it," she says, "the way that light blinks—and the faces."

She's watching me, sitting very straight as she listens.

I glance down the hall at Tate. He's distant, but still there. Still watching this.

" 'I think I might love you,' I told him." I turn back to her.

"You did?" Her eyes are glassy.

"Yes. I never told a boy I loved him before."

"Oh," she says. She's holding her hands under her chin, listening.

"And, this is the part I will never forget—"

She nods—she wants more of the story. Her hands have moved up to her cheeks. She's blushing.

"He smiled—like I'd told him something wonderful. And his hair fell into his eyes—you know, the way it always did?"

Yes, yes. She remembers. She holds her face in her hands.

"He brushed his hair away from his eyes, like this—" I brush my hand along my forehead. "He had such beautiful eyes."

"Yes," she says. She is looking past me, to a place where she can see them.

"And—he took my hand by the fingertips." I show her with her hand. "And then—"

"What?" Her eyes are bright and wet.

"He kissed my hand. There." I point to the top of her hand to show her. "He said, 'You didn't need to tell me. I always know when somebody loves me.' He knew," I say.

Richy's mom nods again, tears streaming.

"That was Richy. You never had to tell him," I say.

"He just knew," she says. "You didn't have to tell him."

After Richy's mom leaves, I'm still on the bench. I feel Tate next to me as he sits down, but I don't look at him.

"If I hadn't used up all my words, I'd tell you thank you," I say. "I—" I look at my hands. "I thought it would feel better, you know?"

He nods. "I do." He sounds sad, too. "You think something might bring them back," he says.

And then something in me understands what's changed. Something in me begins to speak. "In the car this morning, you said I reminded you of someone—who's gone. I don't want to make you remember anything that hurts, but—"

"It was my sister. Maggie." I hear him let out a deep, quick breath.

I do the same.

"She was younger, but she was a lot like you," he says. "She would have stolen Emily Dickinson's dress *in a heartbeat*."

I can feel he's looking at my face, so I let my eyes look up at him.

"That's a joke only you would really get. You know that?"

I nod.

"She was fifteen—way too young for what she was into. It happened so fast. One day she was Mags and she was beating me at basketball, and the next day . . . She was so *angry*."

"What—happened to her?"

He leans over. It's like something heavy is sitting on the back of his neck and he's tired of carrying it.

"She was under the radar by that point—it was always just our mom with us in Pennsylvania and our dad was in Ohio. It was so easy to lose track of her . . . And that night, the night she—she was at a party. It was about this time of year, and she wandered away—or ran away—and she fell into this little stream." He looks up. "It wasn't like she was swimming in the ocean or anything. It wasn't even deep. It didn't make sense."

"I'm sorry," I say. I lift up my hand and reach out to touch him—it's the kind of thing people do—but my hand stays in the air, floating.

"My mother was a wreck, and I said I'd clean out Maggie's things."

I watch him press his eyes shut. "I was fourteen and I thought I was above it all, and then I was inside her head. It was—" He stops. I hear it in his voice, the cracking inside him. "There were her sweatshirts and her trophies and her old toys and the crushed

M&M's she always had at the bottom of her backpack. It was like being inside her mind. Only she—was gone."

"I can only imagine . . ."

"You can do more than imagine," he says. He looks at me, his eyes a direct line to mine. "There was this poem she wrote—I found it. About walking into water—I never told anyone about that poem."

"You think she—?"

He sits up straight, suddenly. "Doesn't every fifteen-year-old write something that says . . . ?"

I shrug. "I don't think I'm a testing ground for the typical," I say.

An elderly couple walks past us. Something has happened to them. They seem to be caving into each other. I watch them as they pass, holding each other up. "What you said about—" I stop.

"What?"

"You think I'm like her. I have *that* in me?"

"At first," he says. "I thought so."

"*Oh.*" I feel my shoulders collapse.

"But then you broke my nose."

I did? My heart's whirring suddenly. "And"—I swallow—"*then?*" Wings in my chest flutter, close to my heart.

It's quiet, but he seems jittery. He's shifting on the seat. "Then I saw—what you had was different."

I feel my eyes squinting at him. "Different?"

"The way you see things—it's not sad. It can be very funny."

"So *that's* what you saw after I broke your nose?" My heart slows. "That I see things in a funny way?"

He laughs. "Not funny as in odd, funny as in you can still see some light in things—no matter how dark they are. I knew that no matter what happens, that part of you won't let the rest take over." He looks into my eyes. "You *won't*."

I feel my eyes stinging.

"Claire—" He leans over to me, the little crease between his eyes. His eyes make me think of water. He's trying to pull me in toward him, but I won't go.

"I thought you were going to say you knew something else," I whisper. It's all I can manage. I blink and the stinging stops. I look at my feet.

"What?" he asks quietly. He leans closer. I can't see this, but I can feel it.

"I thought you were going to say . . ." I pause. "That you found out I had a good right hook."

I hear him laugh.

"So I have the whole view now," I say, nodding for a long time.

"And what do you think?"

"I think—" I stop. I keep my eyes on the floor. It's better that I try not to look at him—not even his hands—anymore. "I think it's a lot to see in one day. And, Tate—"

I take a long, deep breath.

"I can see how much you miss her."

Now I can see.

I look at the gray wall. "Did you ever think . . ." I do manage to look in his direction. I avoid his eyes. "Maybe I should just mail it the way it is?"

"Hmmm?"

"Her dress. They'll be happy just to have it back. That will be the most important thing to them. Why don't I just put it in a box and mail it the way it is?" I manage to look at him.

He raises his eyebrows. "I guess you've just had me convinced that it would somehow be wrong."

Chapter 26

I'm in the back of Grace's van with Tess. It's late. The grown-ups up front are going back to a house I'll live in for a little while longer before I disappear, leaving almost nothing behind.

We dropped Tate off at his car near the Innernet, where we left it what seems like years ago. I know he's somewhere on this same highway, going in the same direction as I am, but separately. I know that's the way things will be. I try not to look behind us.

No more looking for him on rivers, either. A solemn vow.

Tess leans over and whispers, "So?"

I lift my eyebrows.

"Tate?"

I shake my head. "You said the question was why would he follow me. And now I have the answer. He thought I was another sad story."

"Hmmm?"

"He followed me because he thought I was like his sister, who died. He was trying to save me."

She shakes her head dramatically. I see her mouth make a soundless *What?* She shrugs, and she puts her big arm all the way around me. "Well, you're not. And we're graduating in a few months and moving on. Nobody's going to stop that."

I put my head on her shoulder. "There is still the little matter of a dress in my closet," I whisper.

She nods. "What are you thinking?"

"When we get back, I'm finally going to tell my dad. Tomorrow, first thing." I feel her hand on my head. I move my hand up and give hers a squeeze.

"Isn't there some other way?"

"No," I say. "It's really time."

When I wake up, it's Amherst, my room I know. But this room, my room, is different, changed from the outside in. I wonder about that, how a room can change overnight. Same butter-colored walls and the same way my mother's books make a fort of protection—she's here protecting me still, but I'm different. The beginning of a new person. Just the outline, I know, but someone else.

I move toward the closet and kneel on the floor. I take the first of her books and smell her lavender.

> *I thought I was invisible until*
> *I saw in a mirror, myself, raising my hand.*

I take the second and the third book, and stand and walk to the empty bookshelf under the window.

Until I felt that hand touch my cheek, I thought
I was something like the sky, blank and blue and
in the background.

My mother's books fill up the first shelf and spill over to the second.

Now they are *my* books.

I thought I was buried alive
until I felt myself taking root
and then I heard myself say
there must be another name
for what I am.

I move back to the closet and hold on to the doorknob. I lift the hanger from the bar and leave this room with it, walking carefully and holding on tight.

I can hear my father opening the front door. It's Grace. The air carries the scent of the earth up the steps, along with the cool air. As my foot crosses the top steps I hear just a few of his quiet words to her.

"What would I have done without you?"

It's just me and the dress for the last time.

I hear the top step creak. I lift the dress just over the banister rail as my father and Grace turn toward my voice. They look up at me like they are happy to see me.

"Grace, I'm glad you're here." I hear a stranger's voice come out of my mouth. And then one that sounds a little more like mine. "I need your help."

I watch as their faces turn from happy to awestruck to confused.

I know later I won't remember walking down the steps holding Emily Dickinson's dress.

My father's face is unnaturally white. He seems to have foam at the corners of his mouth.

I turn to Grace. "I can't tell if he's breathing. Grace, is he?"

"Of course I'm breathing," my father spits out. He narrows his eyes. He seems to be part catatonic, part evil supervillain. I'm pretty sure this is a side of him that's new to Grace, too.

"Put that dress in the dining room before it gets any more *damage*," my father manages to say while grinding his teeth. I especially hear the way he grinds out the word *damage*. It's only slightly odd that we agree the damage is the worst part.

He turns to me. "You have committed grand theft. Do you have any idea what that dress is worth?"

I swallow. Somehow I manage to get to my feet.

"Dad, please sit."

"Do you know how much trouble you are in?"

"Yes, of course I know. Please, sit. *Please*."

He backs up and sits, perfectly straight—a mighty oak I stand in front of. I take a deep breath. "We never say this—to each other—but I love you." My voice is shaking. "And today I need you very much."

His face is still solid.

"I could have put this dress in a box and mailed it," I say. "I might have gotten away with it. But I didn't do that. I want you to know why I didn't do that. I want you to know why I have this dress in the first place. It took me a while to figure it out myself."

I watch as Grace awkwardly finds a spot on the periphery.

"I was alone with my mother on three days when," I start.

My dad flinches.

"The third time—" My voice gives way, planks of dry wood, a rickety footbridge. I swallow again. My mouth is so dry. "I kept the dress this long because—" I try to clear my throat. "I was trying to—" My voice gives out on the last word.

I feel something warm on my cheeks. Wet. The corners of my father's lips are changing.

"I started to think about Emily Dickinson," I say. I feel hot, hot wet tears. "And somewhere in the middle of that—" My vision is flooded. "I found Mom." I can't see my father clearly anymore. "I needed to find her—"

Then my knees start to buckle.

"I wasn't ready to say goodbye." I feel the floor give way and I fall through the footbridge—down, down.

I am on my knees, sobbing. Long, circular sobs—unstopping, rotating sirens. Tears in a hot downpour. *After years in the desert.*

I've waited so long, stopping is not an option.

The animals in the room have changed.

I have used up all my tears and just the hiccups remain: crying that isn't quite done. I feel a bear paw on my back. It's warm and patting me. It wants me to do something. There's a bird here, too, persistent and high-pitched.

I start to open my eyes. Grace is the bear. Her other hand is on my arm.

"Your father," she whispers in my ear.

I slowly unfold my body from my knees, look up. My father is the bird. He has wrapped one arm around his head so tightly it looks as if he is a man with an elbow for a face. The sound he makes hurts my ears and deep inside my chest. It's the sound of things that will always be partly broken.

Grace says my name. She motions with her head toward my father.

I manage to stand.

I am next to my father, but I don't know what to do. It's as if I were a baby raised in the forest and now I am brought into the world where people stop speaking sometimes and touch. No one has shown me how.

I understand how to put my hand on his head.

When I do this, I release some kind of spring, because the arm around his head catches me and pulls me to the ground and then I am surrounded by arms. I am kneeling and my father is holding me very tightly.

"So, so, so sorry," he sobs.

Chapter 27

IN SPRING, AMHERST CHANGES into a storybook. The students grow wings from their heels and run through town spinning and singing. You get the idea that some parts of life are pure happiness, at least for a while. The toy store in the center of town puts all its kites outside on display so that the tails and whirligigs can illustrate the wind. Grace has asked to meet me at the Amazing Bean. Whenever I imagined my life, I never expected my father's girlfriend would be asking me out for coffee or that I would be walking through a town about to burst into blossom, but here we are.

"I should have asked," she says, "if you liked coconut. I know I have a lot to learn about you." She moves a small plate with two cookies covered in coconut over to me. "For some people it's a deal breaker." She looks at me and then quickly away and then back. Her eyes are the color of blueberries and they are flecked with other colors. Like Gus's glass. She looks away again, and then back again. When she does this, she makes me think of butterflies.

So I take a cookie. It crumbles all over the tabletop as I take a bite. "I—um—I'm not going to eat alone, am I?"

I watch her pick up a cookie, and then she shuffles around in her chair. It's like she can't quite get comfortable. "Your father doesn't know," she starts, "that I asked you here."

"Is it about the dress? Is it—"

"No. The dress is all set. Restored and perfect and the Dickinson people were just happy to have it back. A fraternity prank and the Smith professor who was the intermediary. It's over."

As she says that, I look out the front window of the Amazing Bean. Some kind of tree has let loose its blossoms in the wind. The petals swirl upward and sideways. "It looks like snow," I say, remembering the day in January with Tate.

It seems like more than four months ago.

Grace turns. "Thank heavens it's not." I hear the bell on the front door.

I look toward the door. Expecting . . . ?

"Do you see him?" she asks. "S-sam? He hasn't been around—"

"Hmm?" I turn back. *I'm trying hard not to,* is what I should tell her. I just stare at the table.

"Sorry. None of my business." Her hands disappear from the table.

"No," I say. "It's just, you know—time to move on. To think about what comes next." I shrug.

She tilts her head and nods. "Moving on," she says. "I think you're right about it being time." I see her duck and reach out from under the table. She lifts up a large, flowered gift bag. "A graduation present. Your father doesn't know anything about this. It's from me."

I look at the bag, see the lime-green tissue paper peeking over the top.

"I keep asking myself if it's all true, if it's possible that I'll have a life after high school."

"It's more than possible. It's happening."

I look up at her, at her face, how convinced she is by the words she's saying. "And anyway, a sad memory about an article of clothing shouldn't eliminate that type of clothing from your wardrobe forever. Your father would disagree, which is why I didn't tell him anything about it."

I feel my eyes wrinkling.

"Just open it."

I reach into the tissue paper.

I unfold the paper. "A leather jacket?"

She nods. "Vintage, of course. It has a good story to go with it—I know about your friend Richy and his jacket. But that's the past." She reaches across the table and touches my hand. "I think it suits you. I also know your father will hate it."

I pull my arm through one of the sleeves. "Yeah, he will. But I love it."

Emily Dickinson's dress is back at her house, and Grace is invited to the reception. Grace and my dad want me to go to the celebration. My dad, especially, wants me to see the dress in the house.

"You can come back here anytime you want," he says. *"During normal business hours."*

We are walking up the long driveway. Grace is in a flowered green dress that makes her auburn hair seem stunning. My father can't keep his eyes off her. Grace agreed with me that it wasn't too warm for a leather jacket, even though I really know it is. I put my hands in the pockets, and follow one step behind.

Everyone is small dots blending in and out of the garden, so you can't tell the people from the flowers, like in an Impressionist painting. I am watching the way things blend and shift. At the top of the driveway, I watch Grace flow into the trees. My father follows. He can step into another place as long as she takes his hand.

But here I stay: there's a frame around their world, and I'm on the opposite side, watching. And it's almost time for me to leave, to find my own place I can step into.

I will find it.

So you could say, *That's how the story about her dress ends.*

You could say that.

But—

Chapter 28

"YOU LOOK—" THE VOICE, AS USUAL, comes from behind me and makes me shiver.

He's in a dark blue suit, with a white shirt and a paisley tie. "Very bad-ass," he says. I'm warm already in my black leather jacket, so it doesn't take much to make me blush. "It's perfect," he says, nodding.

I push my hands deeper into my pockets.

But I don't look away.

It's okay to look at him now, from this distance of time and space. I just stare at his face, seeing what might have changed. I don't even care that I'm blushing. I know I won't see him after this—the dress is back and out of our hands—but I'll want to remember his face, the way it changes all the time.

I don't want to forget that part of the story.

"You look—very grown up." I smile. I look specifically at his eyes. It's a color you never see.

He looks at me, then at the dappled scene in the garden, at all the poetry people in their party clothes. He seems to have caught a conversation elsewhere in the scene or maybe just in his head.

"I'm—uh—starting to pack . . . for India?"

"India?"

"I told you, right? I'm going for eight months. I was sure I told you."

"You never really told me"—I allow myself to let out one sigh—"much."

"It's all complicated," he says, looking away. I can't hear what he says next. I think he says "with you."

It's the kind of thing I'm not sure I want to clarify. I just allow myself to stay distant. Hands in my pockets, feet on the ground. But he won't seem to let me. His voice gets urgent. He wants to rope me back in. "You said you wouldn't do anything *without telling me.* You promised."

He's looking at me in a new way—it's a loaded look, like he's telegraphing me news from the underground, important news that might change the outcome of the war.

"It had, you know, *reached the expiration date?*" I shrug, and manage to stay in my separate orbit. I know about orbits now. *You are not pulling me back into yours.*

"I ran into Grace," he continues in that voice. "She told me about this party. I wanted to be here—because—"

He starts to say more about the underground, maybe to explain that they're low on food or to talk about morale—something cryptic and only partially honest. He doesn't get a chance. A man dressed completely in white—some sort of historical reenactor—appears right next to us. He looks oddly familiar, with very heavy white eyebrows and a white mustache.

"The two of you," he says definitively. It seems like the answer to a question on a game show. But what's the question?

"Oh—yes. You were our tour guide in September," Tate says. Another answer, but this time I know the questions are: Who are you? And why are you dressed like that?

The man with the eyebrows lowers his head, and his voice is meaningfully hushed. "I recognized your picture right away."

There is a self-conscious pause while someone passes by. The conversation is taking on the characteristic of secrets again. "It's hard to believe that story made it all over New England." Tate says this but seems to be asking something, too. He's looking puzzled.

"When I saw the picture on the news, I instantly recognized the two of you." He chuckles.

"You did?" I'm looking at his face. He is quite amused, his eyes twinkly. There's something in that look that doesn't correspond to the story of the murder of a boy in Rhode Island.

"The back-door video camera never turns off even though it's very blurry. But you'll remember, probably, there was a full moon. Seeing the two of you again—it was unmistakable."

Again?

"I said, oh, it's really them, but now they're in Providence and they're crime solvers. I said, *What kind of people are they?*"

He continues, but the hair on my arms starts to rise. *Back-door video? Moonlight?* Tate's still confused, I can see.

"What are you? Secret agents or something? What did you need the dress for?"

On the word *dress*, the hammers start—in my head, my throat, pretty much all over. I see Tate's mouth drop open.

There is a video of us running. Strike that. Make it *there are two videos of us*: one when we were running from the photographers in Providence, and another one. Here. Running from Emily Dickinson's house.

Oh.

"Are you going to arrest us?" I ask. I'm leaning forward, almost touching the man's face with mine.

"Heavens, no," the man says. He waves his hand through the air. He almost bats me with it. "I made the connection weeks ago. We have the dress back. It's perfect. Story over. But here you are." He giggles. "I just can't believe it's the two of you."

"I don't understand. Why aren't you calling the police?" Tate says. His face is red, his eyes big and round.

"It's Emily Dickinson," the man in white says, still hushed. "*I know.* She had that effect on you, too. It's like enchantment." He sighs. "Anyway, I'm glad you came to the party."

We are laughing so much it's hard to stand upright and cross the street. It takes the two of us a long time to stumble over to the town common. We sit on the grass under a big maple tree. When the laughter stops, it gets quiet.

I hear myself breathe in deeply. "It's good to see you," I say, "looking so nice." I really mean this, and I'm glad I can finally say it.

"So." He leans back, his arms behind him. He crosses his ankles. "Your father—and Grace—did they help?"

I nod. "I have people to help me," I say, "when I need it. And I know how to ask for help—now."

He's looking at the grass near his hand, studying it carefully. You could even say *monitoring* it.

"Do you remember," I say, "when I met you at Emily Dickinson's grave in September? You were running through in an Amherst College shirt."

He nods. "I do. Of course . . . It's been a long, strange trip." He laughs.

"I wish—" I stop, because orbiting this is easier than being in the middle of it. But then I start again. I put myself on the same planet next to him. I speak because I won't ever get another chance again and I know what that really means.

"It's too bad it's over," I say very quickly. "This will make you laugh. I wish we were still in the middle of it. That I still had the dress. Do you believe that?" I laugh. It's a sad laugh, but I try to make it seem happy. I'm afraid to look at him.

I'm very afraid to do that.

"Then it shouldn't be over," he says.

What shouldn't be over?

"Hmmm?"

"My brother, Ben, is here. Helping me move some things out . . ."

"Uh-huh."

"Yeah—I'd, uh, like you to meet him."

"You would?" I ask. *Meet your brother?*

"Tomorrow," he says. "We can tell him all about the dress. He'd never believe me."

We?

Tomorrow?

The light comes through the trees in beams. I can hear the water. I don't know why I'm here, walking behind them.

"So why does Claire call you Tate?" Ben asks. The three of us are out in nature.

"I was the student teacher in her English class," Tate says. "You know that already."

"So what are you now?"

Tate laughs. It has an echo. It floats around the forest. "Ben's into labels. Tell Ben about Tess's game," he says. We stop by the water. Dragonflies are circling.

"Game?"

"You know—the one where you have to say 'human or dancer.'"

"Oh," I say. "You know that song—are we human or are we dancer? Tess has made up this thing where you say what you think people are. So this is how it goes: Human or dancer?"

"Oh, I see. So what's Sam?" Ben asks, nodding toward Tate. Tate throws a rock in the water.

"Human, definitely human," I say.

"Ooo. Sorrrry, dude," Ben says.

"It was different before I broke his nose." I laugh, but it's really pretty true. After that day, he was different.

"What about me?" He looks at me. He is equipped with everything Tate has, only he's the dark one, with extra sculpting and curly chocolate hair. It can be hard to speak when he asks you a question.

"I don't know you—"

"This game is based on personality?" Tate asks. "Now I *am* hurt."

"Of course it's not the same game once you know someone," I say.

"Can labels change? I thought that's why they're called labels . . ." Ben says.

Ben sits on the rocky bank near the river and crosses his legs. He motions for me to come, too. "Okay, I want to play. On first impression, then?" Ben is very good at flirting. Is this some kind of test? Is that what I'm here for?

"Let's see," I say, sitting next to him. "On first impression? It's an inexact science, you know . . ."

He nods.

"You are an unusual case . . ." I say.

His dark eyebrows rise.

"*You* are both."

Ben collapses into me. "Yesss."

"What? That's in the rules?" Tate's laughing, but his voice is remote. He's standing off apart from us. He seems to be farther away than I'd noticed.

"You're going to Swarthmore next year?" Ben says. "I'm at Penn. I'll show you around Philly. Come for the weekend. You can stay in my dorm."

Out of the corner of my eye, I see Tate turn and walk toward the creek.

Then Tate's gone.

Crash. Glass in shards, everywhere. Three large tumblers, all wiped out on the tile floor.

My dad comes running into the kitchen, trying to unscramble the intentional from the unintentional.

"Just an accident," I say, "involving glass. Nobody's dead."

Ah. It reminds me. *Dough Buddy's dead.*

"It hurts." I say this out loud?

"Are you hurt?"

"No."

"You look . . . wrong," he says.

"Tate just confused me."

"What?"

"He introduced me to his brother. And then his brother invited me to stay in his dorm at Penn."

"What?"

"It's not—I'm not going to do it."

I hear him exhale. "Good." I look up at him. He's looking a little odd, moving his arms around like they're not comfortable. "The *staying-in-his-dorm* thing," he says. "I mean, get to know him first."

"Huh?" I feel my face tighten.

"I mean—do you *like him*—the brother?"

"He's a little . . . uh . . . advanced for me."

"He's even *older*—?"

"Not that kind of advanced. He's like nineteen or something. What do you mean *even* older?"

My dad looks at me. He's about to say something, but he's giving it a lot of thought. "You and Sam . . ." he says. "This thing . . . between the two of you."

Swallow. Breathe, slow and regular. *"Thing?"* I say. It breaks coming out.

"I'm not blind," he says. "That first day, when you showed up, with his blood in your hair—"

"Yeah, I got it, Dad, I remember that day," I say, but this does not stop his progress with the sentence.

"You would never give me any kind of straight story. And I knew he was a college student, so I figured it was a crush."

A crush? Is that it? Tate thinks I've had a crush on him?

"But then," he continues, "when you were talking to Richy's mother at the police station I saw something else. He wouldn't take his eyes off you."

He was watching Tate watching me?

"There was something . . . *there.*"

"A loaded God complex?" I offer, remembering the look on his face when Ben said to come to Philly for the weekend. "There was never anything worth mentioning, really. I never kept anything from you. I just—I remind him of his sister," I say. "She's . . . gone. He's like a lifeguard." I can feel the emptiness of that in my chest. "Anyway—it would be too weird—with his brother."

I look at the broken glass. "It's over now. I'm moving on." I nod in a big way to show him I really mean it. The glass, I can see as I do this, is scattered all over the room. We'll be finding shards in strange places forever. That's what happens. "Dad?"

"Yes?"

"You and Mom," I say. "Was it like you and Grace?"

He shakes his head and exhales one long breath. "Grace is very special to me. Very special." His fingertips touch his mouth. "But your mother . . ." he says, looking off, somewhere distant, where he sees her. "You only get *one* of those."

"I was just thinking that's probably the way things go," I say.

He comes close to me and puts my head on his chest. He puts a hand on my head and sighs.

Yesterday, I said goodbye to Emily Dickinson's dress. And today I said . . . what did I say to Tate? More important, what was he telling me?

Not much.

It's warm outside, but the metal bench is still holding on to winter, still cold. I lay my head on the arm of the bench and feel the chill deep inside. The paint is peeling. It feels like spikes on my cheek. I close my eyes and listen: all the birds have returned and the wind shakes the new leaves.

Then I hear someone sigh.

"Claire."

Oh. Not again.

"I don't—" I keep my eyes closed, but I can feel my heart start racing. "Just because I prefer humans doesn't mean I have a crush on you."

And then I don't hear anything. I crack my eye open to see if he's disappeared the same way he appeared. The sun leaks in and I see there's something there, big and dark, blocking the sun.

"I know," he says. I close my eyes again and hear him. "I know the difference, and I think you do, too."

I feel myself pressing my eyes closed. "I keep thinking I've seen you for the last time," I say, "and then you reappear."

Silence.

"Why is that?"

"I came to see your father."

I don't open my eyes.

More silence, but I know he's there, the way he blocks the breeze, the way he shifts and his clothes softly sigh.

"Right. You like to tie up loose ends. I know that much about you anyway," I say. "But they're all tied up. Happy ending. You were at the party."

"I have to tell him I was there that night—with her dress."

"Why?"

"Because I know you didn't."

"So?"

Then he's silent again. And I hear just birds who are busy and nervous.

"I hate when you do that," I say.

"I'm sure you could mean that about a couple different things I do."

I open my eyes and see his face, backlit by the sun. At first he's all golden from the angle of the light, but then I see his face is scratched. He's got blood streaks by his nose.

"What happened to you?" I stand up quickly, looking closely at his face.

"Nothing."

"*Nothing?*" I move closer and take a good look at his nose. It's red and swollen. I look at his face—all over it. Even banged up, all I can think of is how good it is to see his face. How right it feels to have his face here— and the rest of him, too. How much I don't want him to leave again. "Maybe there's some force in the world trying to get your nose back to the way it was and make you just the way you were before I met you."

"*That* would be impossible," he says, sitting on the bench.

Then I feel something tighten in my chest. The tightness travels all the way up my throat. "I can't do this—" I feel my hands making fists. "I can't." I start to feel small explosions in my temples. I think I might even see sparks. "*That would be impossible?*" I hear my voice start off high and screechy. It's a bad beginning, and then I hear my words get lower, louder. "I don't know what you mean. Do you know how tired I am of that? Do you know how tired I am of not knowing what you mean?" I feel my eyes start bulging. I feel how stiff and straight my back is. I can't seem to stop myself from speaking. "*Who are you?* What's your middle name? What are you going to do in India? What's up with your dad? What do you order on your pizza—"

I feel his hand grip my arm. "I had a fight," he says suddenly. "With Ben."

"You and your brother have fights where you punch each other? *What kind of people are you?*"

He raises his eyebrows and looks at me. "Uh, are you sure you want an answer to what kind of people punch other people?"

"Hhh." I cross my hands over my chest and look away. I look at the pine tree, which I notice has a collection of mushrooms at the base of the trunk. I focus on them. I notice half a robin's egg.

"We don't usually punch each other."

I sit on the bench next to him. I let out a long, deep breath. The mushrooms, I notice, are so ironically cute they seem like storybook mushrooms. Not far from this bench seems like a good place for elves and wood nymphs. If I weren't so upset, I would point this out. "And that blow to the head convinced you that you need to talk to my dad about the night we—*I*—took the dress?"

"No—it didn't convince me to say something about the dress. I would have told him even if Ben didn't punch me. I mean—I only found out that it was back in the house yesterday, and I couldn't say anything at the party, and I wanted you to meet Ben—" He closes his eyes and shakes his head. *"It was about you."* His eyes are still closed.

I wait for what feels like a full minute. "What?" I ask finally.

"The punch." He glances up at me and then looks away. "I told him he was out of line. I mean, really—'*stay in my dorm*'?"

I find myself shaking my head. "Sorry, I'm a little lost here. You were offended because he said I could stay in his dorm?"

He nods very slowly, still not looking at me.

"Tate, I think this big-brother thing has gotten a little out of hand, don't you? I'm not really your little sister, and it was your—"

"That's what he told me. After I punched him and he swung back. He said this isn't about Maggie—" He looks up at me. "But I already knew. I knew when you broke my nose."

I watch him, the way his face seems to change with every sentence. "You knew I was funny. I remember. You told me that."

"I didn't finish. I didn't tell you—everything I knew."

"Huh?" I would ask more, but I'm having some trouble breathing. I can feel my heart beating faster. "Then tell me now," I force myself to say. "*Please.*"

I watch his eyes shifting. It's like he's seeing the conversation that's going on in his head. And then he stops and looks at me, right into my eyes.

"I didn't tell you that I knew it wasn't—about helping you. It hadn't been about that for a long time, actually. Maybe it never was . . ." His voice fades out and he looks away. "Claire, *it wasn't about helping you.*" He looks back. "It was about *knowing you.*"

Now there are birds in my chest, and some blankets and pillows and other things that take up a lot of room and press on my heart. It's beating hard, and the birds want out.

"*Me?*" It's all I can manage.

"Yeah. I'm sorry."

"Sorry?"

"I've been trying really hard to stay away. I thought it was better that way. I've been doing that from the beginning. Avoiding you."

"You did a bad job," I manage to say. It is getting hard to speak.

"I know." Does he laugh?

"You promised you wouldn't do anything without telling me and—"

"I couldn't take it to college with me—"

"But as long as you had the dress, we—" He stops. He covers his face with his hands. I watch his fingers cut through his hair. "*We* had something," he says, "together—as long as you had the dress."

"We—we solved a murder together," I say quietly. I squeeze my right hand with my left hand. I squeeze hard. "We'll always have our murder case."

He looks at me. "I'm not joking. Why are you?"

"Oh." I look away. I squeeze my hand harder. "That's what I do—when I'm scared."

"I know," he says. His voice is very quiet. "I know that about you. Already. And—I am, too."

"You are?" I breathe out.

He looks up at the sky. Waits. I see his fingers touching his chin. "You and I are in two different categories—almost different *species*. You need to be a college freshman—after everything you've been through, you are entitled to that." The fingers from his chin move closer to his mouth. "And I'm going to teach in India next year—I thought Ben would keep track, let me know how you were doing, and then maybe someday . . . *Big mistake*—" His fingertips cover up his mouth. "I should have known he would see the same thing . . ."

"You and I—" I start. I can hear my voice is shaky. "We could have met in college. I should *have been* in college. If we'd met at a frat party—"

"You wouldn't have gone to frat parties—"

"In the library, then. Or at Emily Dickinson's grave."

He looks over at me.

I smile.

"When you spoke about the poem that first day . . ." He drifts off.

"About death." I feel my fingers touch my chest, right where my heart is.

"About *life* and living and what it means to make a choice—because *you'd thought about it.* Everybody in the room was listening. It was *instant.* I said, 'Oh.'" He shakes his head.

"You said 'oh' that day?" These words squeak when they come out. I'm having trouble understanding these words. How could words like this be true? My fingers press my heart. My whole hand does.

"Yes. It scared me. It still does. It never stops scaring me." He doesn't look at me. He watches the trees. "And then when I found out how vulnerable you were, how much you'd been through . . . I said no, no . . ."

He leans forward on the bench, so it's mostly his shoulders I see. Then he sits up, suddenly, facing me. He says, "Do you remember in the car, before the memorial service at the zoo? You told me that everybody in Providence would always think you were a carrier of death—that they all would see you that way forever. I wanted to say *you have me.*"

I feel my eyes stinging suddenly.

"But I couldn't."

"I remember," I croak, "that day. Even though you didn't say it. I hoped."

"You did?"

"Yes. I did. *More than anything.*" Now I feel tears.

He lowers his head and looks up, under the shelf of his eyebrows. He smiles, but it fades. "But I can't do that to you," he says.

"You can't do what to me?"

"With you—"

"With me?"

"Ugh. *Do you see what I mean?*" Some large bird interrupts him. It seems to echo his question. He's leaning over, his elbows on his knees, his head in his hands. All I can see is his hair and his broad back.

"I'm going to India and then, next year, I'll graduate. I kept telling myself that. You're going to college. It'll be years before we're . . . *in the same place* . . . years . . . But then . . . I watched you at that police station, with Richy's mother." He turns to me, a kind of emergency on his face. "You had that *magic* with her." He stops, turns away. "I understand your power . . ." I watch him press his hands together. *"Words."*

I wipe my eyes with my sleeves.

"I said to myself, *You will never, ever find another Claire.*" He still doesn't look at me.

I want him to look up. I lean closer. "Do you know," I say, so quietly it's barely a whisper, "the first time I said that about you?" I sniffle. "In the car. I had just broken your nose, and when you thought I was crying." I cough. "Ooh, it has to matter that we're *already good friends.*" I hear my voice get louder. "Why would being in different places overrule that?" I ask, but it's not really a question.

Now he's folded over, his forehead firmly planted on his hands, his elbows on his knees.

This is all finished somehow, a story told in past tense? How do you come to the end of a story without a middle? Without a beginning?

"So it's—*we're*—doomed?" I ask. I hear thumping. Someone's hammering a roof.

Tate takes a deep breath as he sits up and leans against the back of the bench. He slumps, a sail with all its wind gone. He looks helpless. His body seems abandoned on the seat.

It's like a brainteaser: two people on a bench, but just one lost cause.

My heart slows like a wheel that's winding to a stop. It's very quiet except for the words in my head: *a story that's over before it ever got started.* I rewind them and play them over in my mind until what they mean becomes self-evident and irrelevant, like the fact that I must be living to think about life. So I stop.

I feel more tired than I have in a long time, my hands glued to the seat, my head, big and unreasonably hard to hold up. Before I know it, my head is resting on his shoulder, marooned there, immovable.

Tate is frozen. Still.

I can't hear either of us breathing.

I feel him start to move, slightly. I expect he'll pull away now and leave. But then I feel his cheek on the top of my head and he is breathing again. I can hear it. Steady, slow.

On the bench, between us, his fingers lightly touch my hand. Then his whole hand covers mine.

Ah.

It's quiet in the little garden. I close my eyes and hear the wind moving the leaves and the sound they make, like slips under pretty dresses. Like whispers.

Like prayers.

I hear, so far away, the squeak of the front door. When I open my eyes, I see my dad, touching the bridge of his glasses. We sit up quickly, detaching, rearrange our hands at our sides.

"It's okay," my dad says, holding up the palm of one hand.

He's nodding as he turns to leave. "I'm going to get dinner."

"Professor Salter—" I hear Tate's voice being pulled back into the normal world. It's still rusty. "I took the dress," he says, "too."

"Ah." My dad chuckles. "The accomplice comes forward?"

"The *partner*," he says clearly. "It was a mistake—a *mutual* mistake."

"Right," my dad says. "I figured you were involved. Very valiant to come through with this admission, though. Better get some ice for that nose, Claire." He turns. "Hope you can stay for dinner in any case. Grace and I need to settle the bet about how long it would take you to share the responsibility with Claire. Grace won . . . She suspected you wouldn't last." His voice fades. I hear wind chimes, little bells.

And then I am not at all surprised when something about the two of us refolds. My head on his shoulder. His cheek on my head, and all this—the green paper leaves, the perfect mushrooms, the blue of the hatched egg—all this makes perfect sense.

"This is what doom feels like?" I ask in a very small voice.

A big breeze blows in with noise. Far-off thunder?

"No." The trees shiver. And I feel my lungs fill up with the wind. I say it again. "No—I'm not—giving up."

"What?"

"One year. And then we rethink location."

"A year—is still a long time," he says.

I know how long. I know what can happen in a year.

I know that life is an unpredictable ride, sometimes through terrible weather. I know that half of it you don't control. You take that part on faith and say, *Up ahead, things will get better.* You say, *Somehow things will work out.* But I know this, too: the other half is something you can change.

You say, *I have this power.* You say, *I certainly do.*

I rest my head on his shoulder. It's starting to feel like a familiar place now, a place my head might belong. I know, now, what Emily Dickinson meant about hope—how it's a thing with feathers—how you hold on to such a thing. I cover his hand with mine this time. I hold on tightly. "I'm not losing anybody else."

I hear him let out a deep breath. "It's not something you can . . . You're sure you want to try?"

"Yes." I feel my head fill up with air. I could almost float away. "Are you?"

"No. Not at all."

I sigh and some of the air escapes.

But then I hear him. *"Jules, teaching fifth grade,* and *plain,"* he says quickly, certainly. "I don't think you can improve on the beauty of simple tomato and cheese."

"Huh?"

"Those questions. Before."

"Huh?"

"Middle name, what I'll do in India, and pizza preference—the one about my dad's going to take longer."

"We have time," I say. "Don't we?"

"I think we do," he says. He exhales decisively. "Yes. We have time."

I squeeze my eyes shut. "*Jules?*" I ask.

"My mother's French."

"Oh. Good to know," I say. I allow my hand to reach up to his face. I lightly touch his nose. "That's something I've wanted to do for a long time," I say. "I should go get that ice now."

"Um," he says, "not just yet . . ."

Author's Note

I definitely have a thing for writers' houses. I see a *place* as irrevocably tied to the spirits who spent time there, especially a place those spirits loved, and I doubt anyone was as connected to a place as Emily Dickinson was to her home. She grew so homesick after her first year at Mount Holyoke Female Seminary, just ten miles away from Amherst, she didn't return even though she loved her classes. If you ever get the chance to visit her house, which is open to visitors, you might understand Claire's attraction to it. You will not get to see her original dress—as Claire does—but you will see an identical replica. The original white dress is on display at the Amherst Historical Society. I saw the original dress many years ago, and the writing of this story began there and then.

Who knows what Emily Dickinson might have made of such interest in the everyday stuff of her life? Maybe she would have laughed. Maybe she would agree with Tate, who expresses doubts at the beginning of the book about the wisdom of taking a writer's private life and making it a tourist attraction. I doubt she would disagree with me, though, about how some part of the essence of a life—the spirit—might be absorbed by the wood and stone of a place, how that spirit is something you might feel when you are there, especially if you need to feel it. It's as Claire says: *A house remembers*.

Acknowledgments

This is one of those books that took a village. First, from the Amherst village: Thanks to the folks at the Emily Dickinson Museum, who make sure that special house will survive. And in support of their Replenishing the Shelves Project—with hopes of bringing back to her home all the books that inspired Emily Dickinson (www.emily dickinsonmuseum.org/books). Next, I need to thank my agent, Elizabeth Kaplan, for her faith in the story, for her persistence and patience my first time out—and for using the word *love* in regard to manuscripts. Much gratitude to everyone at Roaring Brook, including copy editors Karla Reganold and Janet Renard, and jacket designer Timothy Hall. Special gratitude belongs to Nancy Mercado, my editor, who, in addition to being a genius, also has X-ray vision. She detected something in a very different story and took a chance. She stripped it down to the floorboards and wall studs and then helped me rebuild. Nancy is truly my partner in writing this story.

I thank everybody who supported me and never let me give up—Mary, Taline, Laura, Susan, Tinker, the Class of 2012. I can't forget the important young people in my life who inspire me every single day—my writing students at Boston University. Colin and Catherine, you planted the seeds of this story, each in different ways, and I am grateful. Thanks to my family—you are the reason I tried to do this in the first place—especially my sister Joni, who sustains me in every way possible; my husband, Paul, who always said this would happen, even when I didn't think so; to my children, Yoshi and Mack, who, every day, show me how much joy there can be in the world: a lot.